MICHELLE LYNN ROSS

Signed, Sealed, Delivered

FAWN
CREEK
PRESS

For every teen mom who doubted she could, but went ahead and did it anyway.

Acknowledgments

Thank you so much to my friends and readers for all your love and support. When I first started this series, I just wanted to tell a story that felt like home—for the small-town folks, the dreamers, and of course, the Kansans.

I never imagined that so many of these characters would start speaking to me, each one insisting they deserved a story of their own. Your excitement and encouragement for every new book mean the world to me—you're the reason these characters get to live and love on the page.

Even though this four-book series is complete, Fawn Creek isn't done with us yet. There are still so many people in that little town who deserve their own happily ever afters, and I can't wait to bring them to life.

A special thank you to Allison for tracking down the Nee-wollah parade lineup and solving that little mystery for me, and to Jess for finding the photo so I could see the beginning for myself. And a huge shoutout to my ARC readers—Billie, Christian, and Dala—your support means so much.

And finally, to my husband—thank you for listening to my endless ideas (even when you've heard them a dozen times) and for always cheering me on so I can bring these stories to life. Thank you for all you do to help me chase my dreams.

Prologue

"Hey. It's okay. Mommy's here," I say to Piper, my screaming six-week-old daughter, as I bend down into the crib to scoop her into my arms. "Let's get you some breakfast." With my baby snuggled against my chest, I make my way out of our bedroom and down the hall to the kitchen.

"Here you go," Zach says, stepping into the hall, holding a fresh bottle out to me with an outstretched arm like a knight in shining armor. Except, it's my boyfriend in his work uniform.

"Thank you." I sigh taking the bottle and offering it to our infant. She latches on immediately and begins to devour the milk as though it's the first meal she's ever had. I take one more step toward Zach and stand on tiptoe to quickly give him a kiss.

"Off to work?"

"Off to work. You girls going to be okay today?" he asks, with a clear look of worry across his face.

"Yes," I assure him, forcing a soft smile. "I have to eventually figure out how to navigate this mom business on my own. Might as well start today."

"I just hate to think of you being alone all day. At least when your mom was home, I knew she could come over and help you. But with her out of town..."

"I'll be fine," I say as I place my free hand on Zach's shoulder. "Piper sleeps all day anyway. I'm going to get her fed and then put her in her bouncer so I can get some schoolwork done. We are going to be just fine."

Zach nods, shuffling his feet nervously. "Text if you need me. My mom can come over, or I can leave work if I need to."

"Seriously. Go. We will be fine. You don't need to be late," I assure him again, this time gently pushing him toward the door. "I love you. Go so you can hurry up and come back home. I can't miss you if you don't leave."

"I love you, too." He groans. "Seriously, text me if you need me."

"I will. We've got this, babe. You and me."

* * *

Piper and I are snuggled on the sofa as she finishes her bottle and gently turns away from it, almost as though to tell me she's lost interest. I lift her tiny squished body to my chest and gently pat her bottom until she lets out a loud burp.

"You certainly are your father's child," I mutter to my tiny infant as I pull her away from my shoulder and lay her in my lap. "Good thing you're cute," I say, stroking her belly as she lays sleepily on my legs.

I pick Piper up from my lap and lay her in her bouncy seat, then move to the kitchen to refill my coffee. Once that is done and her bottle is washed and sitting in the drying rack, I pick up my laptop and make my way back to the living room to start on my schoolwork for the day.

The exhaustion is real. For both Zach and me. Yes, we knew when we found out that we were pregnant that life wouldn't be easy. We were young. Too young. In fact, we were both juniors in high school. I had barely turned seventeen when we had to go to both of our parents and inform them that they were going to be grandparents.

Thankfully, they were supportive. I suppose they didn't have many other options, of course. But they made it clear that we needed to work hard to graduate so that our future baby would have the life she deserved. Immediately, Zach got his GED. His mom wasn't thrilled with his decision to not finish school traditionally. However, his newly acquired diploma did allow him to get a full-time job. A good full-time job, in fact, with health insurance and vacation time and life insurance and an hourly wage of twenty dollars an hour. This job would definitely help us get a good start in life.

I switched over to online schooling. Not that I needed to so soon. I could have finished out my junior year and switched over this year to finish up. But, let's face it. I live in the Bible Belt, right in the middle of the United States, in the tiny town of Fawn Creek, Kansas. In a town of 1,200 people, word spreads fast. Especially when the word is a discussion of two high school juniors who are expecting a baby out of wedlock.

I couldn't do it. I couldn't go back to face my teachers and coaches and fellow students. So instead, I quietly withdrew from school and enrolled in online high school instead.

Zach and I moved into our own place too. Well, kinda. We moved into the apartment above my dad's garage. The room that we once used for playing pool and storing my mom's holiday decorations is now our home. It's a tiny space, but it works for us, and I'm thankful to have my parents close by.

Except today. Today they are on a flight to Seattle to go on a cruise with their friends, and I'm here just trying to navigate a newborn all on my own.

Everything is fine.

I get logged into my Chromebook and navigate to my assignments for the day, deciding to start on my least favorite subject and get it out of the way. Math. I'm just opening the page when there's a knock at the door.

I look at Piper, who is in her bouncy seat, and frown. "Who could that be? All our friends are at school, and Daddy's at work." I climb from the couch and make my way toward the door.

Standing on tiptoes, I peek through the peephole to see a familiar face. Chief Sanders, the police chief of Fawn Creek, is standing on my wooden porch. Quickly, I unlock the wooden door and swing it open, offering him a soft smile.

"Chief, hi. How can I help you?"

The chief's face softens immediately as his eyes bounce from me to Piper. "Ava, can I come in? I need to talk to you."

I nod and step back, allowing his large frame to make its way through the door.

"Is everything okay?"

He frowns, causing the wrinkles around his eyes and mouth to deepen even further. "I think you should sit down for this."

Obediently, I take a seat on the sofa as he sits in the recliner across from me. He leans forward, resting his elbows on his knees while holding his hat, absentmindedly rotating the bill in his hands.

"What is it?" I ask, looking down at Piper, who looks back at me and yawns as though a visit from the police chief happens every morning.

"Ava, it's Zach. He got into an accident this morning."

I shake my head and stand from the sofa. "An accident? I

4

don't understand. He was just on his way to work. I just talked to him. Is he okay? Where can I see him?"

The chief motions for me to sit back down.

"I know. It happened this morning on his drive to work. He crossed the center line and... well... Ava, I don't know how to tell you this, but he didn't make it."

I narrow my eyes. "No, that can't be right. He is a very careful driver. You have to have him confused with someone else."

I dig around the blanket on the sofa next to me and pull out my phone, before scrolling to his name. I hit the call button and put the phone to my ear. "He's going to answer, and I'll show you that you have him confused with someone else."

The call connects and rings on my end, resulting in a ringing cell phone in the chief's pocket as well.

He frowns and pulls the phone from his shirt pocket, offering it to me.

I take the phone and look at the name scrolling across the screen.

It's my name. This is Zach's phone.

He's really gone.

"No," I whisper, shaking my head. "This can't be real. We just had a baby. She's so little. And he loved her so much. He was such a good dad." The tears roll down my face. "What am I supposed to do? I can't raise a baby by myself. We were supposed to do this together. He promised me he would do this with me."

The chief shifts uncomfortably in his seat. "Ava, is there someone I can call for you? Someone who can come sit with you? Your mom, maybe?"

I shake my head. "No. My parents are on the way to their cruise. Oh my gosh, their cruise. It's going to be ruined. They are going to have to come home. They've been planning this for years and saving up. My dad is going to be so disappointed."

"It's going to be okay. They are going to understand," he assures me.

I nod. "Yeah, they will, I guess. What about Zach's parents? Who is going to tell them?"

"I will. I'll tell them."

"And you'll tell them to come here? Or should I go there? I don't know what to do. I don't think I can drive," I ramble. "My car. I can't drive because Zach was driving my car, and the base for Piper's car seat was in there. How will I get her to the doctor? Oh my gosh. How am I going to do anything without a car? How did this happen?"

I groan, my mind racing, and I lean in further to the chief. "You said he crossed the center line? That's impossible. He is such a cautious driver. He pays... paid... dammit... close attention to the road always. He never texts or lets himself get distracted. Something isn't right."

The chief shifts in the chair. His large frame takes up the entire recliner as he leans forward toward me. He lowers his voice. "Ava. I know it's not fair, and I know this is hard, but it was him. We have witnesses who saw the whole thing. They said he looked like he was slumped over. Like he had fallen asleep."

I gasp and slap my hand over my mouth. "He fell asleep?" I look down at my lap and then to Piper, who is now peacefully sleeping in her bouncer. "It's my fault," I whisper.

The chief shakes his head. "No, Ava, it's not."

"But it is. Piper was up last night screaming her head off, and I was so tired. He got up and fed her. If he hadn't been up with her last night, he could have been sleeping, and then he

6

wouldn't have been tired today. This is all my fault. And now I have to raise Piper all alone. What am I going to do?"

Chapter 1

"Piper, it's time to get up!" I say as I lean into her bedroom doorway. "You've gotta get ready for the first day of school."

Piper's eyes snap open at the mention of school, and she jumps out of her bed.

"First grade! Yay!" she squeals as her feet land on the floor and she dashes towards the outfit we set out last night.

"Get dressed and then come down for breakfast. I'll drive you to school today for your first day, and then tomorrow you can start going to school in the morning with Kate."

"Okay. Don't forget to pack my lunch in my new Minecraft lunchbox!" Piper calls out to me as I leave her room and make my way down the stairs to the kitchen.

I warm up a frozen waffle and place a few strawberries on her breakfast plate. By the time her breakfast is ready and lunch is packed, Piper is already bounding down the stairs, dressed and ready.

"Can I have whipped cream and sprinkles on my waffle? And chocolate syrup?" Piper requests as she makes her way into the kitchen and takes a seat at the kitchen table.

"Isn't that kind of a lot of sugar for the first day of school?" I ask with a raised brow.

"It's the same as a donut," Piper argues. "Grandma told me

so."

"You have a point." I shrug as I make my way towards the fridge to get the can of whipped cream. "But this isn't an everyday thing. Just a first day of school thing. Deal?"

"Deal."

I dress Piper's waffle and slide the plate in front of her. Then, I make my way to my leather tote bag that's sitting on the kitchen counter. I pull out my planner and open it to check my agenda for the day.

As soon as I see the date, my stomach flips, and just for a second the numbers on the page blur. *August 18th.* Today isn't just any date. On this date seven years ago, Piper's dad passed away. One minute I was just starting a typical morning, and the next, the chief of police for Fawn Creek was knocking on my door to tell me that Zach was gone.

Every year, I assume this date will be easier, and every year I find out that I'm wrong.

"Mom. Mom. Mommy... you okay?" Piper asks, finally breaking through my thoughts.

I look down at my sweet little blonde-haired girl. "Yes, sorry. I was just thinking."

"About what?"

I shake my head. "Just things I need to do today," I lie.

I can't tell Piper that today is the anniversary of her dad's death. She's too excited. I can't make her sad. Not today.

* * *

We make our way across the grassy lawn in front of Fawn Creek Elementary when Piper spots her best friend, Kate, and her little sister, Kenzi. They are crossing the street, holding hands with their mom, Madison.

"Hey," I say to Madison, closing the distance towards them. "Kenzi, do you get to start school today, too?"

Kenzi nods excitedly while wearing a hot pink kitty cat backpack that's bigger than she is.

"Yes! I get to go to school with my sister now! And Piper. But I don't get to eat lunch here," she pouts.

I nod. "I get it. It stinks that preschool is only a half day, but at least your mom makes good lunches, and you'll get to take a nap at home instead of at school."

"I guess," she replies.

I turn to Kate. "What about you? Are you excited to start first grade?"

"Yes!" Kate squeals. "And I'm so happy Piper's in my class. Maybe the teacher will let us sit by each other."

"Maybe so," I say as my eyes wander across the lawn, landing on a face that I haven't seen in years, not since Zach's funeral.

It's Zach's sister, Emilee. Our eyes meet, and she sends me a half smile.

Last I knew, she lived in Missouri, but apparently she's back and dropping off her own kid for school today. A cousin that Piper barely knows. If Zach were still here, Piper would know her cousin well. But life had its own plans.

I want to go to her and ask when she moved home, but our relationship just hasn't been the same since he died. Ever since then, I've had a feeling that Emilee blames me for his being gone.

In all honesty, I blame myself, too.

"Bye, Mom. We're going in." Piper snaps me back to reality.

"Wait. Don't you want me to walk you in?" I ask, stopping the girls mid-stride as they head towards the front door.

Piper shakes her head. "Nope. We are big kids now. We can go in on our own."

I frown and bend down to give her a hug and kiss the top of her head.

"Okay, if you insist. Have a good day. I'll pick you up after school today. I love you."

"Love you, too!" Piper calls over her shoulder as she, Kate, and Kenzi make their way towards the open front doors of the building.

I watch them disappear, almost unable to believe how grown up she looks.

As the girls disappear inside, I turn to look back at Emilee, thinking that maybe I can still catch her. But she's already gone.

"Well, I guess I'll get back home and wait for my non-school kids to get there." Madison interrupts my train of thought and brings me back to reality. "Have a good day, Ava!"

"You too," I reply with a wave as we part ways towards our cars.

I'm still not sure how I can have a good day at this rate.

But who am I kidding? *August 18th is never a good day.*

Chapter 2

"Good morning!" Cassidy calls out from behind the counter of Drip, Fawn Creek's cute little coffee shop, as I make my way through the door.

"No Piper today?"

"I lost my little assistant to first grade, I'm afraid," I report with a shrug. "Looks like I'm on my own until fall break."

"What are you going to do with yourself?"

"Probably actually accomplish things for the first time in months," I chuckle. "I feel like I've done nothing all summer. Even with her in daycare."

Cassidy smiles softly as she wipes down the counter in front of her. "Well, you were busy. You moved into your first house and made it yours. That's a big deal. Not to mention the fact that your real estate business is booming. You need to give yourself more credit."

"I suppose you're right."

"I'm a mom. Moms are always right," she reminds me with a wink.

"I'm a mom, too."

"Yes. But I'm old enough to be your mom, so I win," she teases. "What will you be having today?"

"Just an iced caramel latte. A big one, please."

"Sure thing! So, what's on your docket for today?" Cassidy calls over the scream of the espresso machine.

"I don't know. I kind of want to go back home and crawl back into bed. Today is the seventh anniversary of the day Zach died." My voice cracks at the admission. "I'm not okay. But I have to be okay, because life is still life-ing."

Cassidy turns to face me with a new softness in her eyes. "Oh honey. I'm so sorry. I didn't know."

I shake my head, fighting back the tears. "It's okay. No one does, honestly. It's not like the rest of the world has today's date circled on their calendar. It's just... hard. I feel like I'm the only one who remembers."

Cassidy finishes making my drink and slides it across the counter. "Maybe you should take the day off today. Sometimes it feels good to climb into bed and rest when you're feeling sad. Spend the day under the covers eating junk food and watching silly movies."

I nod. "That sounds nice. But I have to get some work done today. And maybe that will help keep my mind off things for a while."

I push my debit card toward Cassidy, but she pushes it back. "It's on me today."

"Cassidy. You don't have to buy me coffee just because I'm sad."

She rolls her eyes. "I'm not buying you coffee because you're sad. I'm buying your coffee because I love you, and there's not enough kindness in this world. And I own the coffee shop, so I can do whatever I want. Now go. Just promise me you'll do something for yourself today?"

"I will. I promise."

* * *

"Okay, I'll see you tomorrow morning at ten." I tell the woman on the other end of the phone as I add her appointment to my date book. Tomorrow I will show her a few Fawn Creek properties in hopes that we can get her moved to town before the holidays. "Have a good day."

As soon as I end the call, my friend Sierra pops her head through my open office door. Sierra owns the salon, Fringe, across the hall from me. We both rent space above the cutest little bookstore in Fawn Creek.

"Hey, bestie. Lunch today?" Sierra asks with a soft smile.

"Is this a pity lunch?" I ask with a raised brow, though with a half-smile so she knows I'm not mad.

Sierra shakes her head. "No. This is a 'we haven't done lunch in a while' lunch, so we're going today."

I nod, satisfied with her answer even though I'm pretty sure she's taking pity on me, anyway. "Okay. What time?"

"Now, if you're free. I don't have any other clients until one. I had a cancellation today."

"I'll get my purse."

Within five minutes, Sierra and I are sliding into a booth at Rio Escondido, the local Mexican restaurant. We order our drinks and food before Sierra rips off the band-aid.

"Friend, really. Are you okay?" she asks, leaning forward to sip her lemon water. "Mom told me what day it is."

"Yes, but also, no." I frown, staring off into the distance. "I just feel like I'm the only one who remembers. I mean, I'm sure his family does, but I rarely hear from them anymore. It's like everyone else in my life has moved on, and I'm still that seventeen-year-old girl, clutching a newborn baby and wondering what the hell I'm going to do for the rest of my life."

Sierra nods and reaches across the table to squeeze my hand but stays silent, letting me continue.

"I just hate feeling like this. And I hate it for Piper. This isn't the life I had envisioned for us." I glance at Sierra, trying to fight back tears. "I know we were young, but we had so many plans. We were going to grow old together. We were going to wait two years and have another baby." I pause, swallowing hard. "And I've never admitted that out loud to anyone."

"Oh friend. I'm so sorry." Sierra replies, her own eyes full of sadness.

"Hopefully, the second one would be a boy, and he would love football just like Zach did. We were going to buy a house on the edge of town, and I was going to get chickens and plant a garden."

Sierra smiles softly, taking in my confession.

"I was going to stay home with the kids until they were in school full-time. Then, I'd get a job that would still let me go to school programs and soccer games and be on the PTA." A shaky laugh slips out. "We were going to be that couple, you know... the one everyone talks about. The high school sweethearts no one thought would make it, but we did."

I frown and stare at the wall. "And suddenly that was just gone. You never know when your life might change in the blink of an eye. We are all just one misstep away from having our lives turned completely upside down. I just wish it hadn't been our lives that got all messed up."

Sierra squeezes my hand once more. "Ava, I wish I knew what to say."

"It's okay. There's really nothing you can say or do to make it better." I blink back tears and stare down at the table. "I just miss him. I'd loved that boy since the summer before eighth grade... and I'd known him since the first day of kindergarten. How am I supposed to just go on without him?"

"I don't think there's a right answer, friend. I think all you can do is just wake up every day and keep going. If for nothing else, for Piper," Sierra says softly.

I watch my tears drip onto my jeans. "I just wish Piper knew what a normal family felt like. Some days I feel like I'm doing just fine, and others, I feel like I'm failing her."

"You are *not* failing that girl," Sierra says firmly. "Piper is fun and funny and spunky and kind. She's literal sunshine in child form. And you did that, Ava. Even in the darkness, when you didn't want to get out of bed, you loved that baby fiercely. You made her who she is. And she is amazing."

Her words pierce straight through me, and the tears fall faster.

"Thank you," I whisper.

"You are an incredible mom, and you are doing everything that girl needs you to do. You just have to keep showing up. One day at a time."

Chapter 3

"Mommy!" Piper's voice calls out as she runs across the front lawn into my arms. I scoop her up, holding her tightly, almost as if I'm trying to catalog every sense of the moment so I never forget it.

"How was your day?" I ask as she wiggles out of my arms and sets her feet on the ground.

"It was the best day ever!" she exclaims. "I love my teacher. Kate's in my class, and we got to go to recess three times!"

"Woah." I smooth out her hair as she talks. "That sounds amazing."

"And we had corn dogs for lunch! It was so cool. I love first grade."

"Hey, Ava," Mrs. Blum, Piper's teacher, calls, waving as she crosses the lawn.

"Uh-oh." I glance at Piper, raising a brow. "You didn't get in trouble on your first day, did you?"

Piper scoffs. "No!"

Mrs. Blum, whom I've known since we were kids, chuckles. "Not at all. Piper had a great day. I just wanted to let you know how much I enjoyed having her in class. You have a very special girl, and I know Zach is looking down on both of you with so much pride. You're doing a great job with her."

Her words hit me hard, and the tears I've been battling all day spill down my face once more.

Mrs. Blum's face softens and she pulls me into a hug. In that moment, she isn't just Piper's teacher... she's an old friend.

"Ava, I'm so sorry. I didn't mean to upset you," she says as we pull back.

I wipe my tears. "No, you didn't upset me. That's exactly what I needed to hear today. Thank you."

She nods cautiously but offers me a soft smile. "You're welcome. Piper, I'll see you tomorrow, okay?"

"Yep! I'll be here!" Piper answers happily, rocking on her heels, oblivious to the surrounding emotions.

"Have a good night," I call, taking Piper's hand and leading her toward the car.

"Where are we going next?" Piper asks as we near the street.

"To see Daddy."

* * *

"So, was pepperoni pizza really Dad's favorite?" Piper asks, taking a big bite of her greasy slice.

I nod, stretching my legs on the grass next to Zach's head-stone. "Yeah. With lots of ranch dressing."

"Do you think that's why I like ranch on pizza, too? Because Daddy did?"

I shrug. "Maybe. I like it too." I dip my slice into my container of dressing. "So maybe you got it from both of us."

Piper nods, satisfied.

We sit in silence for a moment, the hum of traffic nearby filling the quiet.

"Mom, do you think Daddy even knows we're here eating

dinner with him?"

I nod. "Yes. I think so. I think he watches over us all the time. He loves us and loves seeing that we remember him."

Piper looks down at her lap. "But I don't remember him."

"You may not remember the moments you had together, but you've seen photos and videos. Remembering him is about keeping him in your mind... remembering he loves you and wishes he were still here."

Piper puts her slice down and climbs into my lap, wrapping her arms around my neck. "Mommy? Are you lonely without Daddy?"

The sweetness in her voice tightens my chest. "No, Baby, I'm not lonely. I have you."

"I just don't want you to be sad." Piper climbs down and grabs her pizza, taking another bite.

Me too, kid. I wish it were that easy.

* * *

"Piper! How did you coat the entire trash bag in ranch dressing?" I call, staring at the mess in front of me. The entire front of the kitchen trash can is coated in the slimy substance.

"I'm sorry!" Piper frowns, peeking into the kitchen. "I was eating one more piece and I accidentally spilled my ranch."

I sigh. "It's okay. Just tell me next time. Messes happen, but they get bigger if we don't take care of them."

"Okay."

"I'll take the trash out and be right back," I say carefully carrying the bag across the house. I'm so busy watching the bottom of the bag so it doesn't leak all over the floor, I almost don't notice someone standing on my porch when I sling the door open and rush outside. In fact, I'm so distracted, I almost run him right over.

It's Eric. The dad of Carson, one of Piper's daycare friends. And by the way, Eric is drop-dead gorgeous. Not that I've noticed... or cared.

"Woah! Sorry." I step back. "I wasn't expecting someone on my porch."

He shakes his head. "It's fine. I just have a package for you." He holds up a cardboard box to show me. "Wanna trade?"

I frown, confused. "Trade?" I squeak, realizing he means the trash bag in my hand. And that he's in a full UPS uniform holding a package for me. I also take note of the short sleeve of his uniform that is pushed up just enough to reveal a tattoo across his bicep. I've never noticed his tattoo before, but I like what I see.

Wait... since when did I like tattoos?

"Sure. I'll take it to the curb for you. I'm headed that way," he offers with a kind smile.

"Oh, no. Piper spilled ranch all over the bag and it's actually all over my hand. You can just leave the box on the porch. I need to get rid of this mess."

I rush down the steps, shaking my head at the awkward discussion as I dump the bag into the trash can, and turn to make my way back towards the porch.

"How long have you been a delivery driver?" I ask, trying not to focus on my ranch-coated hand. "Not to sound like a shopping addict, but I get a lot of deliveries and I've never seen you before."

He laughs. "I've been with the company a while, but today's my first day driving in Fawn Creek."

"Where were you before?"

"Tulsa."

"Gross." I scrunch my brow. "Nothing against Tulsa, but I'd rather eat a leather shoe than drive there all day."

He chuckles. "It wasn't fun, but it paid the bills while I waited for a spot closer to home."

"And then Randy retired," I say, remembering my favorite UPS driver. "No offense, but you have big shoes to fill."

"Oh, I've heard. Everyone loved Randy."

"What can I say? He was the best. After Piper was born, she was the most colicky baby. I had just gotten her to sleep when he showed up to drop off a box of diapers. I saw him and raced outside to catch him before he rang the bell and woke her up. Once he found out we had a baby inside, he promised never to ring the bell again. And he meant it. Piper's seven now, and until Randy retired, he never rang the bell again. Even when we moved here. I miss him."

Eric raises a brow. "Is that your way of telling me not to ring your doorbell?"

I laugh softly. "No, it's fine. Piper doesn't nap anymore. If you ring the bell, I get a notification and can run by to grab packages."

"Noted." He grins. "Well, I'd better get going. Need to get the truck back to Parsons, and you probably want to wash that hand."

"Oh! Yes, definitely." I say, having long forgotten about the slimy mess all over my perfectly manicured fingertips. I watch him make his way back to his truck and then make my way back inside. Closing the door, I pause for a second, resting against the wood.

Of course, my new, ridiculously hot delivery driver thinks I'm a total spaz. Way to go, Ava.

Chapter 4

"Okay, I'll get that email sent over to you right away. Sign the digital copies, and I'll get them forwarded to the seller's agent."

I cradle my cell phone between my ear and my shoulder as I type on my laptop and end the call. I place the phone down on my desk and take a sip of my iced coffee while still clicking through various files on my laptop.

It's just over a week since school started, and life is crazy. Between nailing down the school routine, Piper's dance class, new listings, a multitude of showings, and more emails than I can wade through in between, I am staying quite busy. In fact, I'm so busy I'm barely keeping my head above water.

Just as I pause to take a breath, my phone chimes. It's a notification letting me know that there's someone at my front door. I click on the alert and can't help but smile when the app loads and I find Eric, the friendly UPS man, standing on my porch.

He leans forward and speaks directly to the camera. "Hey. Just dropping off a package, and I thought I'd deliver a joke, too, in case you need one. What would you call FedEx and UPS if they were to merge?"

Eric pauses. For a second, I'm convinced that he's waiting

for me to answer. Does he know I'm watching him?

"Fed up!" he finally replies with a wide, cheesy grin, obviously proud of himself. He points to the camera. "Admit it. You laughed. You think I'm hilarious. Anyway, don't worry because there will be more where that came from. Have a good day, Ava."

With that, Eric turns and steps off the porch, making his way back to his truck, and I'm left sitting in my office feeling flustered over a cute guy and a stupid dad joke.

"Okay, that was kind of funny," I admit out loud to my empty office.

"What was?" a voice responds, causing me to startle.

It's Tyler, who is not only my friend but is also my landlord, and the woman who owns the bookstore beneath my office.

"Someone sent me a stupid dad joke... it was... never mind. What's up?" I ask, hoping to change the subject. I'm not really ready to discuss my tiny crush on the local delivery driver. Honestly, I'm still trying to wrap my head around it.

Tyler holds up a paper bag with the TBR logo stamped on the outside. "Piper's new Mo Willems book came in today. Fresh off the UPS truck. I thought you might want to give it to her after school today. I know she's been looking forward to it."

The mention of the UPS truck causes heat to rush to my face. He was here, standing in the store below me a little bit ago, and I had no idea. I admit I wouldn't have minded accidentally running into him again.

I smile and take the bag from Tyler after she crosses the room to hand it to me.

"I already paid you, right?"

She nods. "Yep. You are good to go."

I pull the book from the bag and look it over. "She's going to be so excited. She has been obsessing over this book ever since she found out its release date."

"Well, I know she will have already read it by then, but I am going to read it and a couple of other new books tomorrow during story time. Just in case you guys want to come."

"We will be here. Piper wouldn't miss listening to you read for the world. She absolutely loves you and always talks about how good you are at doing all the voices."

Tyler grins. "I love that kid, too. I've been a big fan of hers ever since the day I met her and she asked me why I didn't brush my hair before leaving the house."

I groan. "That's so embarrassing. I still can't believe she did that."

Tyler waves me off. "She was little, and she was watching out for me. Besides, I'll admit, I was looking pretty crazy that day," Tyler laughs. "Ever since then, she's been one of my favorite kids. She really is one of a kind."

"Thank you," I reply. "She's exhausting, but I wouldn't trade her for the world. And luckily, as time has gone by, she has gotten a little better at keeping her thoughts to herself."

I glance at my phone. "Speaking of Piper, I think I'll go pick her up from school today. I'm at a good stopping point for the day, and I bet she will be excited to get her hands on her newest pigeon book."

"I bet so," Tyler agrees as the bell above the door of the bookstore chimes, alerting her of a customer. "I'd better get down there. See you later!"

I gather my things and sneak out the back door of the building to where my car is parked around the corner, while texting Madison that I will pick up Piper at school today.

It's silly. Madison, is Piper's daycare provider and also my neighbor. I could easily walk next door to get Piper once they make it to Madi's saving myself the trouble of going to the school. But with as excited as Piper was to see me at pickup last week, I sure wouldn't mind seeing that again. I could use her joy today and maybe a distraction from the mountain of work I've been buried under.

* * *

"Mommy!" Piper yells as she rushes across the grass of the grade school lawn and jumps into my arms.

"I didn't know you were picking me up today!"

I hug her tightly against my chest. "I wanted to surprise you."

"Well, it worked! Are we going to eat pizza in the graveyard again?"

As the question leaves her mouth, I quickly look around to see if anyone else overheard her and is judging me from a distance. Luckily, the coast is clear. I don't feel like explaining myself to anyone today.

Of course, that's what Piper thinks we do when I pick her up. That's what we did last time. Piper didn't know last Thursday was the anniversary of her dad's death. All she knew was that we were going to have pizza with him. I didn't want to overshadow her first day of school with the heaviness that day holds.

"Not today, sister. I got done with work early and thought you might want to skip daycare and start your weekend early instead."

"Yes! I want to go home and play on my Game Boy," she

25

admits, "and get in my comfy pajamas and have a yummy snack."

"Well, that sounds like the perfect night," I laugh.

"Just let me go tell Kate bye." Piper dashes toward her friend before I can respond.

That's when a familiar voice calls out my name across the lawn. I turn to find Emilee, Zach's sister, making her way towards me. Her son trails behind her with a Paw Patrol backpack that's nearly as big as he is.

I plaster my best customer-service smile across my face, trying my best to hide the hurt in my heart that seeing her causes me. "Hey, Em. How are you?"

Emilee closes the distance between us and swallows hard, as though she's about to deliver me the worst news of my life. Much like when I had to give her the worst news of hers many years ago.

When I offered to call Emilee to save Zach's mom from having to break the news I had no idea how hard it would be. And I never imagined that all these years later I would still remember the sound of her sobs over that phone line so clearly.

"Hey. I just wanted to say hi." She pauses, looking down at her feet before continuing. "And to apologize. I'm sorry I haven't checked in on you and Piper enough over the years."

"It's okay. Your mom and dad have been great at keeping in touch with her."

Emilee looks at Piper, who is making her way back toward us, but stops short when she sees Emilee's son standing nearby. She smiles at Piper and then turns back to me.

"Yeah, I know, but I feel like a real asshole for not being there for you more."

The kids busy themselves with a game of tag around the

concrete Fawn Creek Prairie Pup statue in the schoolyard, as she stands in front of me, looking defeated.

I shake my head before reaching out to squeeze her arm. "No, it's okay. It was a lot for you, too. You and Zach were so close."

"And that's why I should have had a better relationship with you. Seriously, I feel awful. It was just so easy to ignore everything. I went back home after the funeral and settled back into my life, and I did a terrible job of reaching out to you. You needed people to support you, and I bet you felt so alone. You were basically my sister, and Zach would have wanted us to stay close. I just... I didn't know how to do that while dealing with the pain I was feeling from losing him."

A tear slides down her cheek, and my heart softens. "Oh, Em." I pull her into a hug. "It's okay. I don't blame you. It was hard for all of us, and none of us knew the right way to react."

Emilee pulls back and wipes her face. "Well, that may be so, but now that I know better, I want to do better. We moved back, obviously. We're actually staying at Mom and Dad's until we find a place to rent. And I want to do everything I can to have a relationship with you and Piper... if you'll let me."

"Of course I'll let you. There's nothing I'd love more than that." I pull a business card from my pocket and hand it to her. "Text me later. Maybe we can set up a time to get together for dinner and catch up."

She pauses to look at my card. "I forgot you were a real estate agent. I should have thought to ask you for help in finding us a place."

I beam. "Yes, I'd be happy to lend a hand. I know living with parents is rough."

"Yeah, it is. I'll be reaching out soon," she promises, as she turns to call out to her son, Jacob. I also can't help but notice her pause when she and Piper lock eyes. Piper offers her a shy wave and Emilee waves back.

"See you guys later," she says.

"Sounds like a plan. Have a good night!" I reach out and take Piper's hand. "Thanks for being patient back there."

"It's okay. I like playing with Jacob, anyway. He told me today on the playground that I'm his cousin. Is that true, Mama?"

I nod, squeezing my daughter's hand. "It's true. Jacob's mom was your daddy's sister."

Piper pauses to take in this new information as she stands next to my SUV. "Then why didn't I know him already? Shouldn't I have known him for a long time?"

The sadness in her voice cuts straight through me.

"Oh, baby. I'm sorry," I tell her softly. "It's kind of complicated."

"Did Jacob's mom not want to know me?" Her tiny voice squeaks with the question.

I bend down to Piper's level. "Yes, of course she wanted to know you. It was just hard because Jacob and his family lived far away. They didn't really come back home to visit. Grandma and Grandpa always traveled to see them over holidays. But they're here now, and you are going to get to know them. I promise."

"And Jacob will be my cousin forever?" Piper perks up a little as she asks.

"And Jacob will be your cousin forever," I confirm. "Forever and ever."

Piper smiles, though I can still tell it's a bit forced. I pull her into a tight hug.

"Now, we better get going. I have a surprise for you in the

car."

"Is it my new pigeon book?" Piper grins.

I scoff. "How did you know that?"

She shrugs. "I marked it on my calendar when you told me a new one was coming."

I shake my head. "You are too smart for your own good. You're going to be smarter than me one day, and then I don't know what I'll do with you."

She shrugs. "It's okay, Mommy. I'll teach you lots of things."

I smile as I open the car door for her. "I bet you will."

Chapter 5

"Okay, friends. Thank you so much for coming to story time today. Remember that you get a 10% discount off anything you buy in the store today as a thank you for coming to see me," Tyler reminds the crowd as she stands from her seat on the floor in the back of the children's room of her bookstore.

"Mom, can I get a new book? Please?" Piper begs me almost as soon as Tyler finishes her sentence. She sticks out her bottom lip and holds her hands in prayer position to really drive the point home. I smirk at her dedication but don't immediately give in.

"Didn't you just get a new book yesterday?"

"Yes. But I already read it twice. Mrs. Blum says that reading is very good for me and will make me smarter," Piper adds thoughtfully.

Fine. You win.

"Well, your teacher has a point," I agree. "But, just one book. Nothing else."

"Yippee!" Piper exclaims before turning on her heel and making her way towards the bookshelves lining the walls. I step back, out of the direct flow of store traffic, and pull my phone from my crossbody purse, taking a second to check my texts before I feel a familiar hand on my arm.

"Hey," Emilee greets me with a smile. "Sorry to interrupt."

"No interruption at all," I assure her, tucking my phone back in my bag. "Sorry, I didn't even see that you were here. Tyler is a pretty captivating reader; I guess she had me totally sucked in."

She waves me off. "It's okay. We snuck in late after she had started. And she really is!" Emilee agrees. "I don't know where all of those voices came from, and the reading like she was talking underwater was super impressive. Do you think she practices the stories before reading them to the kids?"

I snicker. "Yes. Yes, I do. It's probably less weird now that she has a kid. I can only imagine that before Molly was born, she had to practice on her husband." The thought of Tyler reading a book to her husband, Andrew, while he sits in his recliner looking bewildered causes me to giggle. "I'll have to ask her one day."

"Please do and let me know what she says." Emilee laughs, looking back to check on Piper and Jacob, who are huddled together in front of a picture book display.

"Hey, while I have you here. I'm sorry to bug you about work on your day off, but do you know anything about any rentals that are available in town? Things are getting a little cramped sharing the guest room at my parents' house with my husband and Jacob."

I wave her off. "I sell real estate. There's no such thing as a day off as far as I'm concerned," I say with a shrug. "Honestly, there aren't a lot of available rentals here in Fawn Creek. The apartments tend to stay full and have waiting lists a mile wide. And the handful of rental houses that are in town tend to stay occupied for a long time."

Emilee frowns. "I was afraid you were going to say that."

"People just kind of move here and then never want to leave."

"Well, that's great for Fawn Creek but kind of crappy for me," Emilee says with a laugh.

I pause for a beat and bite my lip before asking the next question. "So... have you ever thought about buying?"

"A house?" Emilee asks, sounding as shocked as if I just asked if she wanted to help me rob a bank.

"Yes, a house."

She shakes her head. "I don't know. I mean, we have a little bit of money put away but probably not enough for a real down payment," she admits, lowering her voice.

"Have you or your husband ever bought a house before?"

She shakes her head. "We've just always been renters."

"Well, there are plenty of programs out there to help first-time buyers," I assure her. "Send me a text when you get home, and I'll send you the contact information for the lender I recommend. There's no harm in checking into it and seeing what kind of preapproval you can get."

Emilee nods just as Jacob makes his way over to us with a book in his hand. "I found my book!" he announces gleefully. "Can we go now?"

Emilee smiles down at her son and nods gently before turning back to me. "I'll talk to Adam and let you know what he says. Maybe it's worth a shot to at least try. We'll see you later."

"Sounds good. Talk to you soon," I say, waving good-bye turning to locate my own child, who has managed to find three books that she's gripping on to for dear life. I make my way over to her.

"Piper, I said one book, remember?"

"I know," Piper mutters in response. "I am just trying to decide. It's hard. Are you sure I can't have all three?"

I shake my head. "How about you pick one, and we will take pictures of the other two. Christmas will be here before you know it, and people will want to know what to buy for you."

Piper rolls her eyes. "Okay, but I might die if I have to wait until Christmas. I need to be reading a lot, remember?"

I nod. "I remember. Maybe you can do some chores or something to make some money to buy new books."

"Or," Tyler interrupts, "you could bring in some of your old books that you don't read anymore, and I could trade you for store credit."

Piper looks puzzled. "What's store credit?"

"It's where you trade Tyler some of your old books that are clean and in very good condition, and that will help you pay for some new books. In addition to money that you raise yourself." I explain.

Piper nods and looks down at her book stack thoughtfully. "Okay," she decides. "I'm going to get this Jelly and Narwhal book now, and I'll put the others back. But I'll be back for them with some of my old books and some money."

"Okay, now that that's settled, why don't we go check out and go to the park for a little while to play?" I suggest. "It's finally a nice day outside, and we should probably take advantage of it while we can."

"Yes!" Piper agrees enthusiastically. "Let's go."

* * *

"Bye! I'm going to play with my friends!" Piper calls out over her shoulder as she races towards the play equipment in the middle of the park before I can even finish climbing out of my car.

I shake my head and take my time grabbing her water bottle and my iced coffee before following in her path. I fully intend to make myself comfortable at a nearby picnic table so I can catch up on a few emails when I notice a familiar figure already seated in my intended spot. Shooting him a soft smile, I continue my journey in his direction.

"Hey, Eric."

"Ava, hey! What are you up to?" he asks, motioning towards the seat beside him. "Feel free to join me."

Accepting the invitation, I plop down next to him. "Thanks. We just got finished with story time at the bookstore, so I told Piper she could come play for a bit before we head home. It's rare that I have a free Saturday morning these days, so we are trying to soak up every minute of downtime that we can."

He nods. "I get it. This is the first Saturday I've had off in six weeks. Carson has kept me running since the second his eyes opened today. He has a lot to make up for."

"Oh, speaking of your job. I got your joke delivery the other day."

Instantly, Eric grins. "It was pretty good, huh?"

I shake my head but let a small grin show on my lips. "It was... okay."

He scoffs. "It was hilarious. I bet you laughed, didn't you?"

"I might have."

"You did. Just admit it. I'm hilarious. I should have been a stand-up comedian instead of a delivery driver."

"You're awfully full of yourself, aren't you?"

He shrugs. "Shouldn't I be?"

I shake my head. "You're something. That's for sure."

Eric leans towards me. "Well, just know that there are plenty more where that came from. Just you wait."

The sound of his promise causes something to lurch in my chest. I know he's just talking about his dad jokes, but deep down I really do hope that means I'll be seeing more of him.

"I'll be looking forward to it."

"Hey Dad, watch me!" Carson calls out across the park from where he stands on the top step of the monkey bars, interrupting our conversation. Without a pause, Carson grabs hold of the first rung and makes it all the way across the bars before ending up on the other side.

"Way to go, Carson! You finally mastered it! You're getting braver and stronger," Eric calls back to him.

"Can you record me doing it again? To show my mom if she ever comes back?" Carson asks.

The way Carson asks that question breaks my heart. Madison's told me before Carson's mom isn't in the picture, but out of respect for her daycare families, she doesn't share much sensitive information. Not even with her best friend.

"Sure, buddy," Eric says, pulling his phone from his pocket and moving closer. He records Carson doing another journey across the monkey bars, and then we cheer him on before he runs off to join Piper on the play equipment once again.

"Can I ask a really nosy question?" I ask, turning to Eric. "And if it's too personal, just tell me that, and I won't ask again."

"Boxers," Eric answers quickly. "Well, boxer briefs to be exact."

I raise a brow, stunned at his response. "What?"

"Well, I just assumed your question was going to be if I wear boxers or briefs. You said it was a personal question, and that's about as personal as it gets," he answers with a shrug.

I shake my head, mostly because he caught me off guard,

but also because, dang it if this man doesn't have me thinking about him in his boxers. "That's not what I was going to ask." I chuckle.

"Oh," Eric says, leaning back against the table behind him. "Well, anything less personal is probably fine. What's up?"

I pause, glancing down at my lap before looking back at him. "I was just wondering... if Carson's mom comes around much? I know Madison said she isn't really involved, but she tends to not talk openly about her daycare parents, and well, I'm pretty nosy."

Eric chuckles. "At least you can admit you're nosy, that's more than most people can. No, she is not part of his life. When Carson was two, his mother, Briana, decided she just wasn't made to be a mom. She signed over her rights to me, and she left town."

This new information makes me angry and sad. "Seriously? She just left? Does she ever check in on him?"

Eric shakes his head. "Nope. Never. She saw him that one last time and didn't even hug him goodbye. She just left." He stares down at his shoes and pauses. "I really thought she'd be back. Or at least she would call and check in on him, but she never has. She just disappeared into thin air."

"Does he remember her?"

Eric shakes his head. "No, I don't think so, at least. Sometimes he asks me questions, like why the other kids at school have a mom but he doesn't, or if she will ever come back. I answer him the best that I can, but it's still hard."

"Being a single parent is hard."

"Luckily, my parents have been very supportive. They watch him for me when I work weekends, and they pick him up after daycare for me. I don't know what I'd do without them. I don't know how anyone makes it without some sort of community."

I nod. "I get it. Piper's dad passed away when she was just two weeks old and my parents are my rock."

Eric frowns. "I'm sorry, what happened?"

"Car accident. He crossed the center line. He was on his way to work. Piper was a very fussy baby, and there wasn't much sleep going on in our apartment. He was exhausted but doing his best and trying to work to support our family. They determined that he probably fell asleep at the wheel."

"That's really hard, Ava. I'm sorry," he says, reaching out to touch my arm gently.

I shrug. "Thanks. It took me a long time to get over it," I admit. "And I'm probably still not over it completely. For the longest time, I felt like it was my fault. Like, if I could have stayed up with Piper, he could have slept that night and..."

"That is not your fault," Eric interrupts me. "Sometimes really bad stuff happens, but that doesn't mean that someone is to blame. It just means that sometimes life just sucks."

That it does.

Chapter 6

"Piper!" I call up the stairs to my daughter's bedroom. "Kate and Kenzi are in the front yard. Want to come out and play?"

"Yes!" Piper responds, already racing down the staircase. "I love Sunday nights."

Over the summer, I had an idea to start a tradition where Madison and I get together on my porch and have a glass of wine while we catch up. Even though we see each other nearly every day, we are often too busy to just sit down and chat. So, that's where I came up with the idea of Sunday Night Wine Down. Now, nearly every Sunday evening, we carve out an hour to sit on my porch while the girls play so that we can catch up and have a glass of wine. Sometimes we chat about what's going on in our lives, sometimes we use it as an opportunity to bounce ideas off of each other... and other times we just have a much-needed vent session. No matter what we talk about, by the time the hour is up and it's time to get the kids ready for bed, we both admit that it was much needed.

I watch as Piper joins her friends in my driveway, where Madison's daughters have already begun to cover the smooth concrete in a variety of chalk art.

"Well," I say, turning to Madison. "How was your weekend? Have you started wedding planning yet?"

Immediately, a wide grin spreads across Madison's face, and her cheeks blush. Just before school started, Madison and her boyfriend, Bryan, took her daughters on vacation to the beach. While they were there, Bryan, with the help of the girls, proposed to Madison with a message written in the sand. The proposal was romantic and sweet and so well thought out. It is exactly what she needed after overcoming an extremely messy divorce. I just hate that I'll lose my porch gossip buddy when she moves in with him after they get married.

"A little," she admits.

"Any dates set yet?"

She shakes her head. "Nothing concrete. I think we are going to shoot for the first weekend in April, so leave that open tentatively."

"Got it," I say, pulling out my phone and blocking out that weekend on my calendar.

"And while we're talking about dates," Madison adds, "what are your thoughts on a quick trip to the beach in January?"

"The beach in the dead of winter sounds great. Tell me more," I say, taking a sip of my wine.

"Well, Bryan and I were talking about doing a joint bachelor/bachelorette trip to Savannah, Georgia. More specifically, to Tybee Island. I've been dying to go visit and do a ghost tour, and the thought of staying in a big beach house with all our friends sounds way more fun than any other bachelorette party I could ever dream up. I just need to know who all wants to go so I can reserve a beach house."

I nod. "Yes, of course, I'm in."

"Perfect. I'll send out a group chat tomorrow and talk to everyone else about it. There's one thing, though. Everyone is going to have their spouses. Is this going to make you feel weird?"

I pause and look down into my wineglass. "No, not at all. I'm getting rather used to being the third wheel or eleventh wheel or whatever I will be," I tease, elbowing Madison gently. She offers a tight smile.

"Seriously, though. If it's going to be weird, then maybe we should just do separate girl and boy trips."

I hold up a hand to stop her. "Absolutely not. There's no way I'm going to let you change your plans for your bachelorette party in order to protect my feelings. I'm a big girl, and I will be just fine. Besides, maybe I'll have a boyfriend by then and can drag him along."

"Oh, now this is the exact kind of tea that I'm interested in hearing about. Do you have someone in mind for that position?" Madison teases.

I pause. Unfortunately, my brain chooses this exact moment to flash an image of Eric in stupid boxer briefs. I take another sip of wine and shake my head, hoping it clears my thoughts.

"No. I'm just saying that it could happen. That's like five months from now. A lot could happen in that time."

Madison, however, is not buying it. The look on her face makes it perfectly clear that she knows I'm not giving her the entire story. She checks her watch and then lifts her glass, downing the rest of her wine.

"There's something you're not telling me. And I'll get it out of you, eventually. But for now, I need to get these kids home and ready for bed."

"I promise there's nothing to tell. I'm just trying to think positively. If that ever changes, you'll be the first to know." I assure her, as she stands from her seat and begins to make her way down the porch.

"Uh-huh. We'll see about that," Madison calls over her shoulder. "See you in the morning!"

"Night!" I call back as I watch my friend and her girls make their way back to her house.

Technically, I'm not lying. There's nothing to tell... yet.

* * *

Monday morning is chaos, as usual. Piper can't find her shoes, I can't find my keys, and halfway up the stairs at work with hands full of coffee and a cream cheese bagel, and my tote bag slipping off my shoulder, my phone starts to ring.

I enter the key code to unlock my office door and unload my belongings onto the desk just in time for the phone to stop ringing and the call to go to my voicemail. Damn it. So close.

With the missed caller leaving me a message, I take the time to unpack and get settled for the day. I switch on the lights, start my oil diffuser, command my smart speaker to play some music, and take a seat at my desk to eat my bagel.

I've just taken my first bite when the voicemail notification comes across my screen. I hit the play button and grab my notepad to take down any important information while I listen.

"Hey, Ava. It's Em. Listen, I talked to Adam last night, and we are interested in looking for a home to buy in Fawn Creek. Can you text me the contact information for the mortgage company you were telling me about? Thanks, talk soon!"

I hang up the voicemail and click over, saving Emilee's contact information in my phone. Then I text her the info for the lender. After that, I give the mortgage officer a heads-up about her incoming new client and finally finish my breakfast.

Who would have thought that after all these years, I'd be working with Emilee to help her find a house in Fawn Creek? She's four years older than me, and likewise, four years older than Zach was. By the time Piper was born, she had moved to South Carolina with her college boyfriend. She only came home a couple of times a year, but even in that small amount of time, the two of us clicked really well. That is, until Zach was gone. She never admitted it to my face, but as small towns go, I heard mumblings of rumors that she blamed me for what happened. I know that's why she pulled away from me and why someone who I thought of as my sister suddenly wouldn't even look at me at the funeral.

It was okay because I blamed myself, too. Over the past seven years, there hasn't been a scenario in my head I haven't worked through, trying to determine if Zach's death really was my doing. If only I'd slept on the couch with Piper, or in her room, or had Zach stay with his parents... but what Eric said the other day has really stuck with me, too. Maybe no one is to blame. Maybe sometimes bad things happen for no real reason. Not that it makes it any easier. But now, I like where this relationship is headed with Em. Maybe we've both grown up enough to try again. I sure hope so for Piper's sake.

I take a sip of my coffee and scroll through my emails, trying to determine where to get started for the day. Just then my phone pings with a notification. It's my doorbell.

Quickly, I open the app and thank God that Eric can't see my goofy grin from where he stands. I watch as he places the package down next to my door and leans into my camera.

"Morning. Just your friendly UPS guy, delivering packages and charm to brighten up your Monday," he says with a grin.

"Hey, speaking of. Why did the package go to therapy?" He

pauses dramatically, as though waiting for a response.

"Too much baggage," he answers with a chuckle, obviously proud of himself. "See ya, Ava. Hope you have a good day."

I can't help but giggle at the silly exchange happening on my front porch. This guy is just cute and dorky enough to make me fall for him. But am I ready to dive in?

I close the doorbell app just as I get a notification from a new group text. The group name is Tybee Time, and the message is from Madison.

Madison: Hey guys, Bryan and I have been toying with the idea of renting a beach house in Georgia the last weekend of January and having basically a combination bachelor/bache lorette trip. What does everyone think? If we want to book a big enough place to accommodate us all, I need to get one reserved ASAP. We would get there Thursday evening and come home Sunday.

Sierra: Cody and I are in.

Avery: I'll have to see if Derek can take off work. I'll get back to you ASAP.

Tyler: Okay, yeah, let's do it! Andrew and I are in.

Ava: Don't threaten me with a good time.

Derek: I'll ask off right now. We're in.

Madison: Well, that was easy. Okay. I'll get back to everyone with prices during naptime today. Can't wait to drink rum runners, go on ghost tours, and stroll on the beach with all of you.

I heart-react to Madison's text and place my phone down on the desk. Life really can change a lot over the course of five months. I can't help but wonder what my life will actually look like by the time this trip rolls around. Will I be sharing a bedroom in this beach house, or will I just prove to myself that I am indeed perpetually single?

Chapter 7

"Well, are you guys excited?" I ask as I join Emilee and her husband, Adam, on the sidewalk in front of the first house of many that we have planned to look at today.

"So excited... and kind of nervous," Emilee admits. "Honestly, I know we are probably late to the game buying our first house, but we've never lived in the same town for long enough to even consider it. Then, when the mortgage company emailed me back and told me how much we were approved for, I thought I was going to faint."

Adam gives Emilee a side-eye. "But just because the mortgage company says we can afford it does not mean that we need to spend that much," he reminds her.

"I know. I know." Emilee waves him off. "We don't need anything over the top, and that's what I told Ava. We are going to stick with looking at what's in our comfort zone."

"Don't worry," I assure Adam. "I won't drive you to be house poor. The goal is just to look at what's on the market and go from there."

"Sounds good," he agrees.

"Well, let's get started. Just remember, a lot of people have cameras in and around their houses now, so don't say anything that you wouldn't want the homeowner to hear you say."

Emilee raises a brow. "Is that a problem for some people?"

I nod. "Oh yes. One time I was walking a couple through a house, and the husband made some wisecrack about the owners' dog being ugly. I didn't think much of it because... well, it wasn't a cute dog. Turns out the homeowner had a camera and heard him when they looked back on it. The prospective buyers made an offer, and there was a matching offer on the table. The sellers chose the people who did not talk shit about their dog and my clients missed out. It was a hard lesson for everyone to learn. I missed out on a big sale, and the owners didn't get their dream house. So, I try to remind everyone before we go into showings."

Emilee's eyes widen. "Okay, noted. Always assume you're being watched."

I nod. "That's the idea."

"It's going to be a long day," Adam chuckles.

* * *

"Alright, this is the last one for today," I tell my buyers as I meet them on the lawn of the final house that we are touring in Fawn Creek. "This is a four-bedroom, two-bath with a two-car garage. It's recently updated, so there's not a ton of work left to be done. It just needs some personalizing if you choose to do so."

Adam raises a brow. "You had me at two-car garage. But recently updated... does that mean the top of our price range?"

I shake my head. "No, actually. This house is listed for $95,000, which is $20,000 less than the last house."

"Thank God," Emilee says. "Not that we would have ended up with that one anyway after Adam announcing to the doorbell

46

camera that the price was highway robbery."

Adam's face turns red. "I'm sorry. I really have tried to keep my mouth shut."

Emilee shakes her head. "It's fine. I loved that house, but the size of the mortgage made me nervous. I know back in South Carolina, homes cost much more than they do in Kansas. But still, the thought of buying a house for over $100,000 makes me queasy."

I nod with understanding before directing them toward the house. "The market has definitely changed. I'm sure it won't be long before you can't find anything decent for under $100,000. As a bonus," I point to the house down the street, "that white house is mine. Piper and Jacob could play all the time."

"And it would be nice to have a friend nearby. For both Jacob and me," Emilee adds.

"Well, hopefully this is the one, then," Adam perks up.

"Well, let's check out the garage and see if it is," I tease.

After a tour of the garage, the backyard, and the downstairs of the unfurnished house, I take a break at the kitchen counter and check messages while Adam and Emilee tour the upstairs.

"Oh my gosh, Ava. This place..." Emilee trails off. "It's perfect. There's room for Adam to have an office and a room for baby number two." She rests her hand on her still very flat stomach, and I raise a brow.

"Does that mean what I think it means?" I ask.

Emilee grins. "Yes! We aren't very far along, so it's a secret."

"Congratulations. That's amazing."

"And that's why we need to get out of my parents' house sooner rather than later," Emilee admits, wrapping an arm around Adam's waist. "We love them and are so thankful they let us live with them, but we really need to be in a house before the baby gets here."

"I get it." I nod in agreement. "Piper and I lived in my parents' garage apartment for six years after Zach..." I stop as I watch the look on Emilee's face change.

It's terrifying how fast a casual conversation can turn to sadness. I watch her transform right before my eyes. One minute, she was excited about bringing a baby into the world, and the next, I'm reminding her of her dead brother. It's like her heart broke all over again.

"Emilee, I'm sorry. I didn't mean to bring him up and make you sad."

She shakes her head, wiping away her tears. "No, it's okay. This kind of thing is bound to happen. Honestly, I have done a lot better for years, but moving home has brought a lot of memories to the surface that I didn't realize I hadn't come to terms with."

We sit in silence for a moment, the weight of the memories hanging between us. Then Emilee reaches out and squeezes my hand, her grip steadying us both.

"You did nothing wrong. He was part of your life, and his loss is part of your story. You deserve to talk about it without feeling like you have to protect me."

"Thank you for that," I say, just above a whisper. "I think sometimes I need that reminder."

"I'll remind you as often as you need," Emilee promises.

"Okay, you two. Are we all good?" Adam asks.

Emilee and I nod in unison.

"Good," he replies. "So, what do we think about making an offer on this house?"

* * *

I kick off my shoes and collapse onto the couch, pulling a nearby throw blanket over me. It's the Thursday before Labor Day weekend and after spending the morning looking at houses with Emilee and Adam, plus writing up an offer over lunch, I spent the rest of the day putting out for sale signs, updating my listings, emailing agents and mortgage companies, and closing offices for multiple pending closings. Honestly, I'm dead tired and never want to get off this couch again.

"Mommy!" Piper calls from the kitchen. "I'm hungry."

Of course you are. Piper, your timing is impeccable.

"Can you make me an omelet?" she asks as I walk into the room.

What kind of first grader requests an omelet for dinner? My first grader, of course.

"Yes, of course. Just a cheese omelet?" I confirm.

"Do we have mushrooms?"

I dig around in the fridge and pull out the ingredients, mushrooms included.

"We sure do. Anything else?"

"Nope! Thank you!" she calls over her shoulder as she skips back to the couch. "I'm going to lay down until my food is ready."

Despite my jealousy of her relaxing while I cook, I get to work. Most kids would request mac and cheese or pizza. Not my kid. She asks for omelets, BLTs, or soup. I joke that Piper has an old soul, and days like today really prove it. Most afternoons she comes home from daycare, puts on her softest bathrobe, and lounges around the house. I wouldn't be surprised if she started asking for a tiny cup of decaf coffee.

Just as I fill the omelet with cheese and mushrooms, the doorbell chimes, and a notification pops up on my phone.

49

"Mom! The doorbell is ringing!"

I place the spatula down and hurry across the house, peeking through the curtain. A familiar brown truck is parked outside and it brings an instant smile to my face.

I fling the door open and catch Eric leaning forward, talking to my camera. His face instantly turns multiple shades of red as he sees me.

"Hey!" he fumbles, handing me my package. "You're home."

"Indeed. I got finished a little early today."

"Oh, I see. Where's your car?" He asks, motioning towards the empty driveway.

I smirk. "In the garage. It's supposed to storm tonight." I explain, before crossing my arms in front of my chest and resting on the door frame. "So? Let's hear it."

"Hear what?"

"My joke of the day."

Eric shakes his head. "Nope. Those are between me and your doorbell camera."

I smirk. "I watch them all, you know."

"I would hope so," he says with a chuckle. "They are hilarious."

"Usually I watch them in real time," I admit.

He places his hand over his chest. "And you don't even bother to say hello? Or good job? Or oh my gosh, you are the most handsome and hilarious man I've ever met? How dare you?"

I shrug. "Maybe I'm not a liar."

Eric gasps. "None of that is a lie."

"Sure," I say with a soft smile, teasing him.

"Mom! Are you burning my food?" Piper calls from the sofa.

"Shit. I gotta go," I tell Eric. "Thanks for the package."

"Anytime, Ava. Anytime." He teases as he turns away from the porch and I hurry back to the kitchen, barely saving a mushroom omelet from setting off the smoke alarm.

As I plate Piper's food, she enters the room, looking up at me with one brow raised. "Was that Carson's dad?"

"Yes. It was."

"Why were you talking like that?"

I furrow my brows. "Like what?"

Instantly, Piper starts to mock me. "Ohhhh... tell me a joke. You're so cute... smoochy smoochy smoochy."

I scoff. "Piper Ann, I did not sound like that!"

"You kinda did," she shrugs. "Do you love him or something?"

I frown. "No. We're just friends."

"Sure. Thanks for the food." She slides her plate towards herself and takes a bite of her dinner, still eyeing me suspiciously.

Is it so obvious that my own seven-year-old noticed I have the hots for Eric?

Chapter 8

"Hello!" Susanne, Zach's mom, calls as Piper and I make our way through the gate into their backyard. Instantly, I'm enveloped in an atmosphere that screams summer.

The sounds of neighbors chatting, children playing, and the smell of burgers and hot dogs on the grill transport me completely. It makes me wish we were just getting started with the season rather than saying goodbye to it.

Piper immediately bolts across the yard to play with Jacob, abandoning me.

"Hi!" I call, carrying a large foil pan of pasta salad. "Thanks so much for inviting us."

Susanne glances down at the pan. "Oh my gosh, that looks delicious," she exclaims. "That pasta salad is thanks enough. I'm so glad you girls came. I haven't hosted a barbecue in years. I think I almost forgot how."

I take in the backyard. Beyond the swing set and trampoline that have always been there for Piper, there's a volleyball net, cornhole game, horseshoes, and enough food and drinks for a small army. "Well, it doesn't look to me like you're out of practice. If I didn't know better, I'd think you hired a professional."

Susanne waves me off. "That's all Emilee. I don't know if you know, but she's a bit of a party planner. I tell her she should open her own business, but... some people are just stubborn."

"I heard that!" Emilee calls as she crosses the patio toward us and pulls me into a hug. "Hey, I'm so glad you guys came. Looks like Piper is already at home," she says, nodding toward my daughter, who is jumping on the trampoline.

"She's good at that," I chuckle. "Emilee, I didn't know you were a party planner. This looks amazing."

Emilee shoots her mom a side-eye. "Well, I'm not... at least not really. I just like to decorate for my own parties. I've never done it for money."

"Well, you should," Susanne says. "You'd make a killing."

"And Fawn Creek doesn't have a party planner," I add. "Everyone has to call people in Owen and hope they're available."

"Does a little town of 1,200 people really need a party planner?" Emilee asks, leading us toward the drink table.

"Yes," I say, picking up a cup and filling it with ice and lemonade. "I hate decorating for parties. You wouldn't have to go overboard. You could offer packages from consulting to full wedding-day coordinating."

"See? I told you so," Susanne says, taking a sip from her cup.

Emilee smirks. "Okay, I'll think about it. Maybe. You guys do remember I'm pregnant and in the middle of buying a house, right?"

"If you wait for the perfect time, that time will never come," Susanne tells her. "Sometimes you just have to start and let the pieces fall into place."

I shrug. "She's not wrong."

"Hey, Mom! Watch me!" Piper yells across the yard before stepping back and throwing herself into a front flip on the trampoline.

"Piper, please be careful," I wince, watching her land on her feet. "She makes me so anxious."

"Daredevil, just like her dad," Susanne says with a grin, elbowing me gently. "But a beauty like her mom."

I smile softly and watch Piper climb down from the trampoline and make her way toward us. "Mom, I'm hungry."

Emilee chuckles. "And she sounds just like her dad."

* * *

Before I know it, it's Monday morning. It's the week following Labor Day, and after a short week, and what felt like a shorter weekend, I'm back in my office and drowning in chaos.

"Hey. Brought you a coffee," Sierra says, poking her head in. "I figured you could use some extra caffeine."

"Bless you, woman," I say with an appreciative groan. "I don't know if there is enough caffeine in the world to get me through this week, if we're being honest."

Sierra plops down in a chair in front of my desk. "Hey, it's a good thing that you're busy, right?"

"Absolutely. This is exactly what I was hoping for when I ventured out on my own, and I am for sure living the dream. It's just... a lot," I admit. "The busier I get, the more I struggle with finding my groove."

"Maybe it's time to hire an assistant," Sierra suggests, taking a sip of her coffee. "Even just a teenage girl who wants to learn the ropes and work a few hours a week."

I put my drink down on my desk and look at Sierra. "Of course! I don't know why I didn't think of that myself." I say, shaking my head. "That's exactly how I got started with real estate, and it would only make sense for me to do the same thing for someone else."

Jessica Weaver, who was a big-shot real estate agent back in the day, kind of took me under her wing when I was in high school. What started out as me filing papers for her and running errands turned into a pretty steady part-time job for all of my sophomore and junior years. Once we found out that I was pregnant with Piper, Jessica made it her mission to get me started with my own real estate career. She taught me everything she knew, and she even paid for me to get my license as soon as I turned eighteen. I thought I'd work for her forever. But then, once she decided I was ready, she announced she was going to retire and move to Colorado. That's just the push I needed to put my plan into action to open up my own brokerage. Now, here I am. Successful, but drowning.

"I guess I'll add looking for part-time help to my to-do list," I say, leaning over to make a note on the notepad next to me. "Thank you. Once I get that done, it will take a lot off my plate and hopefully put me in forward motion away from burnout."

"No problem," Sierra says, popping up out of her seat. "Well, I have a client that'll be in my chair any minute now, so I better get going. I'll let you know if I come across any good candidates for your assistant job. I end up with a lot of teenage girls in my chair. Since they don't bother to hide their phone screens while I'm painting in their highlights, I probably know more about them than anyone else in this town."

"That sounds terrible."

"It is. But it's just part of the job at this point," Sierra agrees. "See ya."

"Thanks again for the coffee!" I call out before turning my attention back to my computer.

I barely get my inbox opened back up when I'm interrupted

by a notification from my doorbell. Quickly, I swipe the app open and can't help but smile as Eric's face fills my screen.

"Ava," he says, as though he is standing right in front of me. "I was getting worried about you. It's been over a week since your last delivery. I was just about to call the police to do a welfare check."

Eric and his over-the-top dramatics cause me to giggle at my phone screen, temporarily forgetting the stress I've been under.

"Alas, thanks to the powers of Amazon.com and the United Parcel Service, I can sleep well tonight knowing that you are safe and sound and throwing your disposable income at what I can only imagine to be more black leggings and random toys for Piper."

I shake my head at the screen, although deep down I know that what he's holding in his hand is a friendship bracelet-making kit for Piper. He's not wrong.

"Anyway, now for today's joke: Why did the UPS man cross the road? Because the chicken across the street refused to sign for your package."

I groan out loud at the punchline and shake my head, but can't help the smile tugging at my lips. This guy is ridiculous, and he knows it. And... it's kinda hot.

Eric pauses and looks into the camera, as though waiting for a response.

"Ava, I know you're watching me. I bet that made you laugh, didn't it?"

Rolling my eyes, I hit the talk button on my app to respond to him.

"Maybe just a little," I admit.

"I knew it," he says with a grin. "Man, you are one lucky girl.

I bet you are the only woman in the world with a remarkably handsome UPS man who brings her packages and amazing jokes."

"I bet you are probably right."

Eric wiggles his brows. "So, you admit that I'm handsome? Nice... we are getting somewhere now."

Once again, I'm thankful that this man can't see the blushing he causes me.

"Don't you have a route to drive?"

"Don't you have houses to sell?"

"I do, actually," I confirm. "Talk to you later."

He smirks. "I sure hope so," Eric says, with a small wave before walking down the stairs. He reaches the bottom step and then turns to look at the camera.

"If you are looking at my butt as I walk away, I just want you to know that I don't blame you."

I shake my head and close the app. I hate to admit it, but I think I like this guy.

* * *

"Okay, I think the only question I have left for you is when can you start?" I ask Courtney, the teenage girl sitting across from me at my desk.

A week ago I told Sierra I needed an assistant. Two days later, she sent this girl over to my office with a résumé and a need to make her own money to pay Sierra for hair and nail appointments. If that's not teamwork, I don't know what is.

"Um, really?" Courtney's eyes light up. "I can start tomorrow after school if you need me to."

Just knowing I have someone in place to tame the chaos of my office puts me at ease. "Perfect. I'd love that. See you around four?"

"I'll be here!" Courtney confirms before heading out.

As soon as she's gone, Sierra pokes her head in. "She's great, isn't she?"

"Yes, you were right. I think she'll be a huge help."

"Next step? You're going to have to let go of a few things," Sierra reminds me. "Nothing that risks your clients, just little things to clear your plate so you can breathe."

I glance around at the piles of paper taking over my desk. "Well, I'm definitely introducing her to filing tomorrow."

"And maybe she can help with social media?" Sierra suggests.

"What's wrong with my social media?"

"Nothing. But it'll save you time. She can make graphics, schedule posts, maybe come up with some reels."

I frown. "I'm not dancing on camera."

"No one said you had to. But I bet if you danced on a kitchen counter or two, you'd get attention."

I shake my head. "I'm not interested in that kind of attention."

"Suit yourself."

* * *

I poke my head into the office. "How's the filing going?"

Courtney's on the floor beside the filing cabinet. A stack of folders sits next to her, already half the size it was when she started. It's only her first week, but my office already looks better than it has in months.

She looks up, her long hair in a messy bun, ripped jeans and a Fawn Creek Prairie Dog Baseball T-shirt making her look effortlessly adorable. I'd look like a train wreck if I tried that look.

"Not bad. Now that I've figured out your system, I think I'm on a roll," she says.

"It looks like it. Thank you for this."

She grins. "Hey, I thought of a reel we could do for your business page."

I hesitate. "I don't know. I'm not much for videos. I'm not a dancer or a lip-syncer."

"No dancing or lip-syncing required," she promises. "Actually, you don't even have to show your face. I just need a photo of a house that's for sale."

"Oh, I've got plenty of those."

"Let me see your phone." She holds out her hand.

I unlock it and hand it over.

She gets to work quickly, only pausing once to hold it up to my face for Face ID before continuing.

"What was that?" I ask, craning my neck.

"CapCut," she says.

"Cap what?"

"It's video editing software."

"I don't think I need all that."

"Yes, you do," she replies confidently, still tapping away. A moment later, she hands it back.

I hit play. The screen shows one of my listings with a funny cutout character raving about the house.

"Okay, that's actually super fun."

"Want me to post it?" she asks with a smirk.

"Sure, go for it."

She takes the phone back, then freezes. "Oops. I accidentally clicked on a notification. You've got someone at your door. Probably just a package." She shrugs and goes back to posting.

"Um, let me check that real quick. Just in case."

I reopen the notification, lower the volume, and Eric's face fills the screen.

"Hey. You did it again. You waited a week to order another package, and you had me worried." He chuckles. "Okay, maybe not worried, but I did miss having an excuse to drop in and talk to your doorbell."

My chest tightens, and I forget Courtney is even in the room.

"The thing that sucks about my hours is that even though my babysitter lives next door to you, I leave too early and get back too late to pick Carson up myself. So instead of me seeing you, it's usually my mom." He leans closer. "And yes, I admit I'm kind of jealous of my mom."

A giggle escapes before I can stop it.

"So anyway, maybe we could hang out sometime? Let the kids play? Or even leave them with Madison a little late so I can swoon you one-on-one with my dad jokes?" He glances over his shoulder, then pulls out a pen and scribbles something across the box he's holding. "Here's my number. Text me when you get this."

He walks away, and I close the app. Only then do I remember Courtney's still here.

She raises a brow. "What was that?"

"Nothing."

"Sounds like more than nothing."

I shrug. "Okay, maybe more than nothing. But how about we move my social media over to the iPad so you can use that for content?"

Her eyes brighten. "Really? Like I'll be your social media

manager?"

"You can make content, but I'll approve it before it's posted."

"Deal. I won't let you down."

"I'm sure you won't." I grab my keys. "Now, I'm going to run a quick errand."

She smirks. "You're totally going to grab that guy's number off your porch, aren't you?"

"Maybe," I admit. "Just maybe."

Chapter 9

"Hey," Madison says, opening the front door to her house and stepping aside. "Piper, Mom's here!" she calls over her shoulder before turning back to me. "How's it going? Come on in."

I kick off my shoes and take a seat on the sofa, just as Piper runs into the room. As soon as she sees me comfortably seated on the couch, she blurts out a quick hi and runs back to Kate's room to continue playing.

"Not bad," I shrug. "My new assistant started this week, which has been an enormous relief. I can actually take a lunch break these days."

"Oh, Courtney, right? Becca's friend."

Becca is the girlfriend of Madison's brother and also Madison's part-time daycare helper.

"Oh, I forgot they were friends! Yes, she has been amazing. My filing is caught up, my inbox is clean, and she's starting to work on social media content for me. I truly feel as though my life is in order. It's like everything is falling into place."

Madison raises a brow. "Good, now that your professional life is under control, maybe we can get your personal life in order too."

"My personal life is just life, thank you."

Madison smirks. "So, is there something you need to tell me then? I saw Eric having a very lengthy conversation with your doorbell camera the other day. Is that an extra service that you have included in your Prime membership?"

I shake my head. "That... was nothing. He's been telling me dad jokes into my doorbell camera when he drops off packages."

"Dad jokes? Um... that is adorable and next-level flirting for sure."

I shake my head. "No. It's not flirting. We are just friends."

Madison rolls her eyes. "Yeah, right. Ava, that guy has had the hots for you since he met you in the storm shelter last spring."

"No, he hasn't."

She smirks. "Oh, but he has. He's hinted around about how cute you are ever since you met. And he asked me a while back if you're single."

I pause. This new revelation definitely piques my interest. "What'd you tell him?"

"I told him yes, of course. I wasn't going to lie to the guy." She shrugs.

I bite my lip and look down at my lap. *He's been asking about me.*

"He left me his number on a package that he delivered on my porch today," I admit.

"Are you going to call him?"

I shake my head. "I don't know."

"Why not? I know you think he's cute. Besides, he's a really good guy and a great dad to Carson. I think it's time for you to get back into the game."

I groan. "Back into the game? It's not like I've been celibate

63

since Zach died. I've dated plenty over the years."

"I know, but you haven't had an actual relationship. Just a lot of dating that was full of dead ends."

"Well, I had more important things to focus on. I've done a lot in the last seven years. I've gotten my brokerage license, opened my own office, bought a house, and raised Piper on my own."

Madison nods and reaches across the sofa to squeeze my hand. "You don't have to remind me how hyper-independent you are. You're a freaking rock star. In fact, you're the true definition of a single mom who is kicking butt and handling things on her own. I'm just saying that maybe it's time for you to let someone in."

My eyes narrow. "That's a lot harder than it sounds."

"I know."

"It's just… falling for someone again scares the hell out of me. Last time I let someone in, I lost him. I don't know if I could survive that kind of pain again."

Madison shakes her head. "Some things are just worth the risk, friend. He could be the one. And you'll never know if you don't try. At least consider it. I think the two of you would be great together."

I let out a sigh and slowly push myself off the sofa. "I'll take it into consideration. But right now I should probably get home and get to work on dinner," I promise before calling out to my daughter. "Hey, Piper. Let's head home!"

Within minutes, Piper and I make our way into the house, and our weekend has officially begun. I drop my keys on the entryway table and pause glancing over at the package Eric left me today. More specifically, reading over the phone number that he left written in black Sharpie.

For a second, I toy with the idea of sending him a text. Maybe Madison's right. I probably am long overdue for a real relationship. And now that I have an assistant hired, I probably could find the time to take a breath and welcome someone new in. But is that what I truly want? I finally got my life into a smooth rhythm. Do I dare throw in the drama of dating and shake it up all over again?

"Mom!" Piper interrupts my thought process. "I'm hungry. Can we have tacos for dinner?"

Looking down at the package once again, I shake my head. As usual, motherhood calls. Searching for my own happily ever after is going to have to wait.

* * *

"Mom, thanks so much for keeping her for me this morning. I shouldn't be gone for more than an hour."

My mom waves me off as she clutches her coffee mug to her chest. She's seated on the couch covered in a blanket, while Piper has already managed to take over the TV in the eight seconds since we walked into the room. "It's fine. Piper isn't a bother, and I have nothing going on today anyway. Take all the time you need. I like having her here."

I nod, fully knowing that I'm going to do my morning showings and then rush back to get my kid. I hate feeling like I'm taking advantage of her. "Okay, Piper, be good. I'll be back in a little bit, and then we will go home and hang out for the rest of the day."

"Thank goodness," Piper grumbles. She's more of a home-body than most adults I know.

I tell my mom and daughter goodbye before stepping out of

my mom's house, just as I get a text from the client I'm meeting this morning.

Audra: Hey, I'm running late this morning. Can we push our appointment back twenty minutes?

Ava: Sure! No problem at all. Let's plan to meet around 10:20–10:30?

Audra: You're the best! See you soon!

Now, with twenty minutes to spare, I decide there is only one acceptable place to visit next.

Within a few moments, I'm pulling into a parking spot in front of Drip. Glancing through the glass window, I can see a few people waiting in line, but nothing that won't be wiped out in plenty of time for me to get a coffee and meet my client with time to spare.

I make my way inside and wave to Cassidy, who is busily taking orders, while her helper, Devin, runs the espresso machine. While I wait, I pull my phone from my pocket and begin checking emails. That is, until the bell above the door chimes alerting everyone inside that someone just stepped through the door. I turn around to see who it is, just in time to watch Eric wheeling a dolly loaded with boxes through the front door. He offers me a soft smile and continues on, pushing the delivery to the back of the shop without another word. Within minutes, he's back, and I can't help but notice the feeling of butterflies in my stomach when our eyes meet. I really like seeing this guy, and from the soft grin on his face, I think he may feel the same.

Maybe Madison's right. Maybe we could be something.

"Here you go, Eric. Thank you!" Cassidy says, sliding a coffee across the counter to him.

"Thank you," he replies as he picks up the cup, "but really you don't have to give me free coffee every time I bring you a delivery. I'm just doing my job."

Cassidy waves him off. "It's not like you drink anything fancy. It's just drip coffee with sugar and cream. Besides, I own this place, so don't tell me what I can and can't do." She winks to show she's teasing. "You take care of me, and this is how I take care of you."

Eric thanks her again, lifting his cup in appreciation before turning towards me.

"Hey," I greet him, suddenly unable to concentrate as I try to find something... anything else to start a conversation about. It's been a long time since a man made me feel flustered like this.

"Hey. I thought maybe you were ignoring me."

I pause, admittedly excited to hear that he's been wondering about me. "Why would you think that?"

He shrugs, glancing across the café towards the front door. "I don't know. I left you my number, and I hadn't heard from you. I thought I might have come on too strong. If you're not interested, then I totally don't blame you."

I shake my head. "No, that's not it. I actually was considering sending you a text last night when I got home, and then Piper asked for dinner and it kind of slipped my mind. I'm sorry."

He raises a brow and a hopeful grin spreads across his face. "So... does that mean I stand a chance?"

"It means... I would be willing to get to know you better."

"That's all I'm asking for. I promise," he says, looking outside again. "But, right now I'm blocking traffic so I better get going. Text me later?"

I nod. "Count on it. I won't forget."

After a busy morning showing houses and grabbing a quick lunch with Piper, we're finally home for the rest of the weekend. I walk into the entryway and drop my keys onto the table as my eyes meet that familiar package once again. This time, however, I type Eric's number into my phone and fire off a text.

Ava: Hey, it's Ava.

It's only a few seconds before I get a response.

Eric: Hey. Glad you got your package.
 Ava: Yep. My new day planner is safe and sound.
 Eric: Good. So, what are the chances I might be able to earn a spot on your schedule?

The straightforwardness of his text admittedly makes me blush.

Ava: Well, I hate to tell you, but it's a pretty rigorous process.
 Eric: I'm up for a challenge if you are.

I pause for a second, considering his text before grinning to myself and texting back.

Ava: You think so? It might take a while. I am very protective of my time and energy.
 Eric: Listen, I don't mind spending my time on things that I know will be worth it.

I stare at his reply with my heart beating rapidly in my chest.

Damn it. Falling for this guy is going to be way too easy.

Chapter 10

"Good morning," Eric says into my doorbell camera when I pull open the app. It's been just over two weeks since we exchanged numbers, and while we've kept up a steady stream of conversation, he's kept his promise not to push me into anything I'm not ready for.

"Just dropping off this box full of what I can only assume is concrete," he says, setting the package down. "You know, if you're going to keep ordering stuff like this, I'm going to have to start hitting the gym or hand in my two weak notice."

He grins at his own joke. "Get it? Too weak?" He shrugs. "You got it. Okay, well, I have a lot of work to do. Feel free to text me and tell me how hilarious I am. I'll probably be back soon with more back-breaking comedy."

I watch him walk back to his truck before closing the app. Then I grab my phone and send him a text.

Ava: It was printer paper. Your joke was cute though.

Eric: Printer paper or concrete slabs? Because that shit was heavy.

Ava: Just paper. Maybe it's time to hit the gym. You seem to be getting weak in your old age.

Eric: Probably. As much as you order online, I need all the

muscle I can get.

I roll my eyes and then realize I'm grinning at my phone like a teenage girl. Thankfully, Courtney doesn't come into work for another hour, so at least I'm not embarrassing myself in front of anyone else.

Ava: I don't order that much.
  Eric: Okay, the fact that I'm at your house three days a week with an Amazon package is just a coincidence. I can't wait to see how often I'm there at Christmas time. But honestly, I don't mind the chance to flirt with you through your doorbell camera as often as I can.

Maybe it's time to have him over for something other than a work call.

* * *

The rest of the week flies by, and before I know it, it's Friday once again. After a busy day full of showings and typing up contracts, I make my way home.

I park my SUV in my driveway just as Eric pulls up in front of Madison's house in his car.

"Hey," I say to him, crossing into Madison's yard from my own. "Fancy meeting you here. And not in uniform."

He waits for me, grinning. "Well, we all get a day off once in a while."

"I always know when you're off work," I tease. "I had a package on my porch today. No doorbell notification. No dad

71

joke. I thought maybe it was you and you were just mad at me... or worse, out of comedic material. So, I pulled up my camera and saw that it was some guy I've never seen before. He just left my package and walked away like he had a job to do."

"Disgusting," Eric mutters as we make our way toward Madison's porch, our footsteps falling into sync like neither of us is in a hurry to get there.

"He clearly had no idea the act he was following."

Eric smirks. "I can't believe you ordered something and made sure it arrived on my day off so you could avoid me."

I hold my hand to my chest, pretending to be in shock. "I would never. Seems to me you knew I had a package coming, so you took the day off."

"And miss a chance to flirt with you through your doorbell? Absolutely not."

I laugh and step ahead of him, knocking on Madison's door. "We wouldn't want that, would we?"

Before Eric can answer, Madison opens the door and gives us a look with one brow raised. "Piper! Carson! Mom and Dad are here," she calls over her shoulder.

Her words cause my stomach to flip and me to freeze in place. *Mom and Dad are here.*

I have to admit, I don't hate the sound of that. Not one bit.

"So, you two are picking up your kids together now. Interesting," Madison mutters to me as Eric crosses the room to gather Carson's things.

I roll my eyes. "We just happened to get here at the same time."

"How convenient," she winks teasingly as the kids come into the room. "Have a good weekend. See you Monday!"

* * *

"Mommy, can I have these extra spiderwebs to hang in my bedroom?" Piper calls out to me as she bends down into a large plastic tote containing our fall decor.

I laugh. "You want to hang spiderwebs in your bedroom?"

"Yes," she deadpans. "You said we are decorating the house for fall. My room is a part of the house."

"True," I agree, "but when I said we were decorating the house I mainly meant the porch and the mantle. Not every room."

"Well, I want my room to be decorated too. I spend a lot of time there."

"Good point. Yes, take whatever leftover decorations you want, and I'll help you hang them up."

"I don't need any help. I'm going to work on my room. Don't come in until I say it's ready."

Before I can respond, Piper barrels up the stairs toward her bedroom, her arms overflowing with fake cobwebs, plastic severed hands, window clings that look like dripping blood, and of course several fake spiders.

Shaking my head, I pick up my phone and fire off a quick text to Eric.

Ava: Oh goodness. Piper is currently in the process of turning her bedroom into a haunted house. She just ran up the stairs with every gruesome Halloween decoration she could get her hands on. She's such a strange kid.

Eric: She's not strange. She's cool. Carson cried last week when he saw a jack-o'-lantern at the store because it was "too creepy."

Ava: Well, better not let him play in Piper's room then.

Eric: Ava... is that your sneaky little way of inviting me over?

I read over the text and feel myself blushing. That wasn't my intention, of course, but I also wouldn't mind if they came over to keep us company. My heart races in my chest as I type out the next text. It's now or never, right?

Ava: Maybe? Are you two going to the parade tomorrow?

Eric: We sure are. Do you want to meet us there?

Ava: Sure, the kids might enjoy having someone to hang out with. And I wouldn't hate the company.

Eric: It's a date, then. See you in the morning.

Chapter 11

"How's this?" I ask Piper as I point to an open spot on the side of the road in downtown Independence. "The parade will come right by here."

"Looks good to me." Piper plops down on the curb. "Do you think I'll catch a bunch of candy today?"

I shrug. "Oh, probably. Not that you need it, since Halloween is just another week away."

"What? I like to have options," Piper reasons. "How much longer before the parade starts?"

"Five more minutes. And keep in mind that after Halloween you will be going through your candy and donating some of it to the Blue Star Mothers. The library collects extra candy to send to soldiers overseas, and I'd really like for you to take some up there after you pick out your favorites."

"Okay, I'll make sure to get some candy I don't like so I can send it to them."

I groan. "Piper, that's not what I meant." Before I can figure out how to explain myself, we are interrupted by a familiar voice.

"Hey," Eric says as he steps up beside us. "We made it, finally. Finding a parking spot was a nightmare."

I watch as Carson takes a seat on the curb next to Piper.

"Same for us. And then I thought we'd never find a place to stand either."

Eric shakes his head. "I get it. Neewollah is the biggest festival in Kansas, so I guess if you want a front row seat to the Grand Parade, it makes sense to stake out your spot early."

"What's knee wall ah?" Carson asks, sounding out the word the best he can.

"It's Halloween spelled backward," I explain. "It's the Halloween festival that is held in Independence every year."

Carson nods, satisfied with my answer.

"And there's a parade with lots of candy," Piper adds.

"This is the first time I've been in ages and the first time Carson's experienced it at all. I forgot how busy it is," Eric admits.

"You just have to keep your eye on the prize. If you survive it all, you get rewarded with a funnel cake." I laugh. "At least that's my reward."

Just then, our conversation is interrupted by the familiar sound of the blank gunshot round telling us the parade is beginning.

"Mom! The parade is starting!" Piper squeals, pointing down the street. The Neewollah color guard is marching our way, carrying the banner that signifies the start of the parade. "Can I have my bag?" she begs.

"Sure." I pull a plastic grocery bag from my pocket and hand it to her.

"Oh, dang it," Eric mutters. "I knew I forgot something. Sorry, buddy. Give me your candy as you get it and I'll put it in my pockets."

Without a pause, I pull a second bag from my other pocket. "Here you go, Carson."

"You're a lifesaver." Eric smiles gratefully.

"You can never be too prepared," I say. "One year, Piper's bag got stepped on by another kid. It ripped and her candy spilled everywhere. We were stuffing our pockets full of suckers and tootsie rolls in the middle of the street. Ever since then, I've made sure to bring extra bags just in case."

"Good call. I have got to get better at that kind of stuff." Eric runs a hand through his hair. "I feel like I'm always forgetting something. I don't want Carson to feel let down because his dad is always dropping the ball."

I nudge him gently with my elbow. "I bet you half the time he doesn't even notice. The important thing is that you're trying. You're not sitting at home or leaving him with your parents when you're off work. You're putting in the work. Everything else is just details, and you'll get better as you go."

Eric shakes his head, looking down at Piper and Carson. "I hope you're right."

I glance at the kids, standing at the edge of the street holding hands, waiting for the parade to pass by. Quickly, I whip out my phone and take a picture.

"I have a feeling that's the first of many cute pictures you'll take of our kids together," Eric says with a smirk.

And I have a feeling he might be right.

* * *

"Okay, kiddos. We have eaten our weight in fried food, browsed every craft vendor in southeast Kansas, and drank nearly a gallon of lemonade. Is there anything else you want to do before we head home?" I ask as Piper pauses in the middle of the street, looking back at the crowd we just left.

"I need to go potty," Carson announces, pointing toward a porta-potty down the street.

Eric sighs. "Okay, Carson, let's go. Be right back."

I watch as the two of them disappear into the crowd before turning back to Piper.

"I just want to do one more thing..." Piper smirks.

"And what's that?"

She doesn't answer. Instead, she points to the sky at the giant ferris wheel towering over the festival and all of downtown Independence.

Immediately, I shake my head. "No way, José. You are not getting me on that ride."

Piper cocks her head and sticks out her bottom lip. "Mom, please? That's the only ride I want to go on. As soon as we do it, we can go home."

"Nope." I stand my ground. "Girl, I don't do heights. You know this. I might pass out or throw up if I go on that thing, and that's going to be a bad deal for all of us, including the guy who gets paid to clean puke off the carnival rides."

"Mom, please? Nothing bad will happen. It'll be fun and we can see the entire town from up there," Piper begs again. "It'll be like flying, except safer."

But I can't do it. Just thinking about being up that high makes me tremble. I shake my head. "Sorry, babe. I just can't."

Piper, obviously heartbroken, quickly wipes the tears from her eyes. "Fine," she mumbles.

I look at her and have to fight back my own tears. I hate it. I used to be braver. Before I had Piper I would have ridden that ferris wheel without hesitation. I used to climb trees and jump into the water below. I used to climb onto the roof from my second-story bedroom window and watch the stars. But now?

Even getting on a ladder terrifies me, much less the idea of a carnival ride.

I know it's not fair to Piper. She deserves to try new things and be fearless and have experiences, but I can't be the one to give her those.

"Hey, you guys okay?" Eric asks as he and Carson approach. "You look like you've both been crying. What'd I miss?"

I shake my head, trying to hide the truth. "We're fine. I think we're just tired and ready to head home."

Piper, however, speaks over me. "Mom's a scaredy cat and won't ride the ferris wheel with me."

Eric smirks at me. "Is that so?"

I sigh. "Yes. It is. I don't do heights."

"Oh, I remember from when I had to save Piper from a june bug last July on the curly slide at the park." he says with a chuckle.

"That thing was creepy," Piper mutters, still staring at the ground.

Eric leans in close, his hot breath grazing my skin and making me shiver just a little. "Want me to take her? Carson won't want to go, but if you can hang out with him, I'll take her."

I raise a brow, glancing down at Piper and Carson and then back at Eric. The fact that he didn't even hesitate to offer makes my chest ache in the best way.

"Really, you would do that? I'll buy your tickets."

Eric waves me off. "It's on me. I wanted to go on it anyway, but Carson isn't a carnival ride kind of kid. You'll practically be doing me a favor by hanging out with him."

I let out a heavy sigh and look down at Piper, who has already perked up after eavesdropping on us. "Want to ride the ferris wheel with Eric while Carson and I hang out down here?"

"Yes!" she replies, bouncing with excitement. "Let's go."

Eric buys their tickets and we all wait in line together, watching the festivities around us.

When it's finally their turn, Carson and I step aside as Piper and Eric buckle into their seat. Then we watch as they float up into the sky.

"Do you wish you had gone up there?" I ask Carson, who is gripping my hand.

"No way," he mutters. "That's too high."

"Same, kid. Same." I laugh softly and take out my phone, recording a video of Piper and Eric as they ride past and soar upward again.

When the ride ends, Eric helps Piper out of the cage and she runs into my arms at full sprint.

"That was the coolest thing ever. You should have gone, Mom."

I glance at Eric, sending him a grateful smile before looking back at Piper. "You know, I'm just going to take your word for it." Then I turn back toward Eric. "Thank you for doing that. It meant a lot to her and me, too."

"Happy to help." He shrugs. "It was a lot of fun."

Without warning, Piper throws her arms around Eric's legs. "Thank you!" she squeals.

"Anytime, kiddo," he answers with a grin.

Seeing how happy he made my daughter makes me want to melt into a puddle on the sidewalk. I'm searching for the words to express my gratitude when Carson lets out a yawn, it's obviously past his nap time.

"You ready for a nap, buddy?" Eric asks him.

Carson nods in response, with another big yawn.

"It's been a busy day and I'm ready for a nap, too." I agree, turning to Eric. "But I'll text you later. I was thinking I might have some more time open in my planner if you're interested."

Eric raises a brow. "Name the time and place. I'll be there."

I bite my lip. "I'll text you when I get home."

"Looking forward to it."

* * *

When we get home, I set down my purse and kick off my shoes. "Piper, I'm going to take a shower and a nap."

"Okay! I won't cook anything or go outside," Piper promises as she heads upstairs to her room.

"Um, okay," I say. I shouldn't be surprised by what comes out of her mouth, but somehow she always manages to catch me off guard. "Thanks."

Still shaking my head at my random child, I pull out my phone and quickly fire off a text to Eric.

Ava: Hey. Thanks again for today.

Eric: No problem. It was fun. Piper's a great kid. Thanks for letting us hang out with you.

Ava: Carson's a great kid, too. Would you guys maybe want to come over for dinner tonight? If you're too worn out from the festival, I understand.

Eric: You couldn't pay me to turn down that invitation.

Ava: See you at six? Burgers and roasted potatoes sound okay?

Eric: Sounds great. See you then.

I toss my phone on the bed, excitement coursing through my veins. I'm really doing this. I'm taking the next step toward dating. And I have no regrets.

Just as I head for the bathroom, my phone vibrates again. Even from across the room I can see it's from Eric.

Eric: Hey, random thought. Have you guys carved pumpkins yet?

Ava: No, I was thinking about doing it tomorrow. I haven't picked up a pumpkin yet.

Eric: How about tonight? I'll bring the pumpkins, you supply the yard?

Ava: I'd love that. See you tonight.

Suddenly, I'm too excited to even think about a nap.

Chapter 12

"Hey, come on in." I hold the door open for Carson and Eric to make their way through. Eric walks in carrying two large, round pumpkins by the stems.

"If you want to follow me out to the backyard, we can carve them on the patio after dinner," I say, motioning for him to follow me. "I was just about to throw the burgers on the grill."

Eric follows me through the kitchen and out the back door, and for some reason, the sight of him standing in my backyard does something strange to my chest. He looks... good here. Like he belongs.

"It smells incredible in there," he motions towards the house.

"Those are the roasted potatoes. They're Piper's favorite, so hopefully Carson will like them, too. Piper's a pretty picky eater, so if she approves, anyone will."

"Carson is definitely not picky," Eric assures me. "He was pretty much raised as a senior citizen for the first few years of his life. He was with my parents almost constantly while I was working nights and sleeping during the day. That is, until he started to go to Madison's daycare."

"That's hilarious. I actually joke all the time about Piper being an old woman herself. My grandma passed away when

83

I was pregnant with her, and sometimes her mannerisms make me feel like she's my grandma reincarnated. It's oddly comforting to feel like I'm raising my grandma, though."

Eric lets out a soft chuckle. "These kids that are raised surrounded by grandparents are built different, for sure." He steps toward me and motions in the direction of the grill. "You need help with that?"

I turn on the propane and throw a couple tablespoons of butter down on the cooktop of my Blackstone before answering. "No, I'm okay," I assure him. "I cook on this thing more than I cook inside the house."

"I admit, I'm impressed. I know it's sexist, but I guess I just don't know many women that grill."

I shrug, admittedly feeling a bit smug over the fact that I've impressed him. "Well, this is a griddle, technically, but I do also have a propane grill in my garage. And an old charcoal grill around here somewhere, too."

"Okay, now I'm very impressed," he admits.

"I love cooking outside. It's fun, it doesn't heat up my house, and it's been a really neat challenge to figure out how to do all of this stuff on my own," I say as I plop the burgers down on the cooktop. "There's been a lot of trial and error, and I hate to admit that I've ruined a lot of food in the process, but it's been a fun journey."

Eric shakes his head. "What are you going to tell me next? That you do all of your remodeling on your own, too?"

"Well," I say, rocking back on my heels as I glance toward the back of the house, "I have learned to do a lot of those things myself, thanks to YouTube. I've changed light fixtures, patched drywall, and replaced caulking. It's been nice to learn to be as self-sufficient as possible. Life is just easier that way."

Eric nods, looking out across the yard. "I get it. It's almost easier to just rely on yourself after a while."

"I'm the one I know I can count on," I admit. "I tend not to let myself down."

"Well, I hope you know there are people that love to help you and be let in. All you have to do is ask."

* * *

"Dinner was amazing," Eric says, taking a seat on the patio next to Carson. The air has cooled off just enough that I pull my cardigan a little tighter around me as I sit across from him. The space on the patio between us is already covered with pumpkins, carving tools, and a big bowl for the guts. The kids flip through the pumpkin stencil book, heads bent together, whispering over which one is cooler. "Truly, I don't think I've ever had such a good burger."

"The secret is the cheese that I stuffed inside of it, and my multitude of seasonings. I'd love to share a recipe, but I just throw stuff together in the bowl until it looks like it'll taste good," I admit.

"Is there anything you can't do?" Eric asks.

I pause for a moment to consider the question. "I'm terrible at keeping plants alive," I admit.

"Me and my dad have a garden!" Carson says, perking up. "Well, we did over the summer. We grew tomatoes and okra and strawberries and cantaloupe. It was so cool and super tasty."

"That sounds really cool," I say.

"Maybe next year you can have a pumpkin patch," Eric suggests. "Last year we tossed our seeds in the corner of the flower bed and grew a little volunteer patch over the next summer."

"Mom, can we?" Piper asks excitedly.

"I mean, we can try. No guarantees that they will make it, though."

"A volunteer pumpkin patch is basically hands-free. Throw the seeds in the dirt and forget all about them," Eric tells me.

I chuckle. "Well, if there's one thing I'm good at, it's forgetting about plants."

"Sounds like the perfect garden for you, then," Eric says before turning back to the kids. "So, Piper. Carson. Have you guys found what you want to do to these pumpkins?"

"I want a unicorn," Piper answers immediately.

"And I want a dinosaur," Carson adds.

I pick up the book and rip out the pages containing the stencils the kids requested. "Perfect. These look nice and complicated," I say, handing Carson's to Eric. "Hope you have all night."

Eric grins. "There's nowhere else I'd rather be."

His words cause my stomach to flip and my heart rate to pick up speed. There's something about the way he says it that makes it feel like he means more than just pumpkin carving. I wouldn't mind if he stayed all night either.

Within five minutes, we have the tops off the pumpkins and a large bowl on the ground between the kids to put their pumpkin guts in. Piper, naturally, is the first to dive in, burying her arms up to her elbows inside her pumpkin.

"This feels so funny," she says with a giggle. "It's squishy."

Carson watches her for a second and sticks one hand in after a little bit of hesitation. He gathers his first handful of pumpkin guts and immediately aborts the mission. "That's so gross. I don't want to do it," he says, shaking his head.

"Come on, buddy. It's okay." Eric coaxes him, sticking his own hand in and pulling out a handful of pumpkin goo to show Carson.

Carson sticks out his tongue and makes a gagging sound. Piper rolls her eyes like she's seen this a thousand times.

"Boys," she mutters. "Carson do you want me to do it for you?"

Carson nods and backs away from the pumpkin, making room for Piper to take over.

While she works on removing Carson's pumpkin guts, I finish the last bit of hers and attach the stencil. "Piper, are you gonna help me cut this out? I got some kid-safe carving tools you can use."

"Yep. I'm going to do it all by myself," Piper answers proudly, making her way back towards me.

And that lasts for approximately ten minutes.

"I'm bored," Piper whines, with her pumpkin in front of her. Her hot pink leggings are covered in pumpkin guts.

"You're bored? You've barely even gotten started," I say, pointing at her pumpkin with only a couple of cuts in it.

"Can me and Carson go play Minecraft?" she begs, tossing her cutting tool down on the patio beside her.

I meet eyes with Eric as he works on Carson's pumpkin.

Carson wanted nothing to do with carving and he's been waiting patiently on the patio, just far enough away to not accidentally touch any guts.

I'm sure when Eric suggested this fun little activity, he didn't plan for it to be just the two of us carving pumpkins while the kids play video games. But I suppose a seven- and four-year-old can't be expected to sit still for long after all.

"Go for it," Eric answers. "We can finish up here."

87

"Wash your hands before you touch anything in the house, please," I call after them as they run inside.

"Sorry. I thought the kids would enjoy this. I always loved carving pumpkins as a kid," Eric admits.

I wave him off. "It's fine. I'd rather we finish them off than make them sit out bored and complaining the whole time. It's been a long day for everyone."

"That it has," he agrees, working diligently on the dinosaur. "I'm really glad you invited us over tonight. It's been a lot of fun."

"It has," I agree. "And the kids have gotten along so well. I'm impressed."

"For sure. I'm sure eventually they'll find things to fight over, but at least for now Minecraft should keep them in line."

I nod, looking down at the pumpkin as I work. This whole night has been so good. Everything I would have wanted for a date, if that's really even what this is.

"Oh, you've got some goo in your hair," he laughs as he crawls toward me. "Hold still."

I do as I'm told, not moving as he inches in close to me, gently pulling the pumpkin string from my hair. "Got it," he whispers, his mouth inches from my face.

And that's when I make my move. No thinking about it. No testing the water. I drop my cutting tool and lean in, gently crashing my lips into his.

He doesn't resist or try to stop me. Instead, he uses his hand to cradle behind my neck, pulling me in closer, deepening our kiss as though both of us have been waiting for this for a lifetime, rather than just a few months.

"Mom!" Piper yells from the house, making her way to the backdoor, causing me to jump back. While I may be ready to explore a relationship with Eric, I'm not quite ready to do it in front of our kids, not until I know for sure that it's actually going somewhere.

"Can we have some ice cream sandwiches?" Piper asks, unaware she just interrupted easily the best kiss I've had in years, maybe even my life.

I look at Eric and shrug before answering. "Sure. Help Carson with his, okay? We're almost done here."

"Okay! Thanks!" Piper replies, already disappearing back into the kitchen.

"That was..." Eric whispers. "I want to do that again."

"Agreed," I answer with a soft smile as he leans in to kiss me one more time. This time the kiss is deeper, longer, more calculated. As we pull apart, I rest my forehead against his.

"We probably better finish up before we get busted," I whisper.

"Oh, Ava. Cute of you to think I'm going to be able to concentrate on anything after you kissed me like that. But I'll sure try."

* * *

"Night, guys," I call out to Carson and Eric as they make their way across the front yard, with their dinosaur pumpkin safely in Eric's hands.

"Thanks for having us," Eric calls back. "We had fun."

"Us too. Let's do it again soon, for sure," I add, hoping that sends the message that I want to hear from him sooner rather than later.

Piper and I make our way back into the house, closing the door behind us. Her unicorn pumpkin is proudly displayed on the front porch.

"Did you have fun tonight?" I ask her.

She nods excitedly. "So much fun. Carson is really good at Minecraft, and he said he likes my house that I built."

"You guys seemed to get along really well. Glad you liked playing with him."

Piper eyes me suspiciously. "So, are you and Carson's dad friends now?"

I nod. "Yeah, we are. So, Carson might come over more often to play if that's okay."

She smiles. "Sure! I like playing with Carson. He's nice and doesn't boss me around like some other people do."

"That's good."

"I like Carson's dad, too," she adds. "He's really nice."

I nod. "Yeah, I think so, too."

I'm just starting to make my way up the staircase towards my room, when my phone buzzes with a text. Expecting it to be Eric, I pull my phone from my pocket and check. It's from Madison.

Madison: Looks like someone might have a plus-one to bring on the Georgia trip after all.

Ava: I don't know what you're talking about.

Madison: Please, you don't get to play innocent. Bryan and I were sitting on the front porch when Eric left tonight.

Damn it. How did I not notice them over there?

Ava: Okay, stalker. So, you should have easily been able to see that nothing happened. He and Carson came over for dinner and to carve pumpkins.

Madison: Yeah, it's not random at all that you had the hot, tattooed single dad over tonight for dinner and pumpkin carving. Just a normal Saturday night.

Ava: Exactly.

Madison: You're pretty much the Fawn Creek welcoming committee. Reaching out to hot single dads to ensure they have a fun and festive Halloween season.

Ava: Good-night, Madison.

Madison: Night, friend. See you Monday.

After finishing my conversation, I toss the phone down on the bed and lay on top of my comforter, staring at my ceiling fan and replaying the night's events in my head. Just then, the phone vibrates again. This time, it's from Eric.

Eric: I couldn't send you to bed without a dad joke... What did the UPS driver say to the hot single mom?

Ava: ...

Eric: If I had known you could kiss like that, I would have gotten on your route a long time ago.

I read over the text from Eric and can't help but giggle before messaging him back.

Ava: Glad I could surprise you. It's the least I could do after you've been such a top-notch delivery driver.

Eric: That's it. I'm letting all the air out of the FedEx guy's tires. I don't need any competition.

Ava: lol. Goodnight, Eric.

Eric: Night, Ava.

I toss the phone back onto the bed and shake my head, still grinning like a fool. My heart is still racing, my lips still tingling, and I have a feeling sleep is going to be impossible tonight.

Chapter 13

It's Monday afternoon, and I'm still riding the high from my pumpkin-covered mini makeout session over the weekend. If anyone had told me a week ago that carving pumpkins could end in me making out with a tattooed UPS driver on my patio, I would've laughed in their face. But here I am, grinning at my computer like a lovesick teenager.

Thanks to Courtney getting both my office and my life under control, I've spent the day flying through emails, scheduling appointments, and getting everything lined up for Emilee's upcoming closing. For once, I'm ahead of the game and the tiny sparkly mood candle on my desk is proof I'm basically a whole new woman.

The door swings open and Courtney clocks in for the afternoon.

"What is going on in here?" she asks, stepping inside like she half expects a jump scare.

"What do you mean?" I glance up from my laptop, pretending I haven't been staring into space replaying a certain kiss for the past five minutes.

She does a slow scan of the room. "It's just so... calm in here. Organized. You've got music playing. A candle. This is not the same dark, chaotic office I usually walk into."

I shake my head. "That's all thanks to you, home girl. You got my files under control, my inbox isn't a dumpster fire anymore, and I can actually see the top of my desk. What's not to appreciate?"

Courtney shrugs her fanny pack off and hangs it on the hook next to the door. "Nope. Something's different. Did you get laid or something?"

My jaw drops. "Inappropriate."

She grins, completely unrepentant, and drops into the chair across from me. "Uh-huh. So I'm right. This has something to do with that UPS guy who flirts with your doorbell camera like it's his side hustle, doesn't it?"

I can feel my face heating. "You are way off base."

"Girl, you're glowing. If you don't spill, I'll just make something up and assume I'm right."

I snort. "You're impossible." I stand and grab my keys. "I have stuff for closing gifts in my car. How are you at making gift baskets? We've got two closings this week."

She smirks. "Teach me, boss. But I expect full details while we assemble bows."

* * *

After an afternoon spent teaching Courtney the fine art of tying cellophane around gift baskets without making them look like crumpled lunch sacks, I hightail it across town to grab Piper from Madison's daycare before she closes for the day and declares me an unfit parent.

As I pull into my driveway and head for Madison's porch, I see I'm not the only one running late.

94

"Hey," Andrew, Tyler's husband, greets me as I step up beside him. "Tyler usually does pickup, but she's running late getting back to town. Do I just ring the doorbell or walk in or...?"

"Oh, Madison keeps it locked so random people can't just walk in," I say with a laugh, knocking as I lean in. His face tightens. "Not that she's had a problem with that," I add quickly. "It's just her thing."

He nods. "Better safe than sorry."

"Exactly."

Madison opens the door, smiling. "Sorry I was elbow-deep in slime. Had to wash up."

"And here I was convinced you were about to throw our kids out and call CPS," I say, shaking my head.

Madison glances at her watch. "It's only ten 'til six. You're fine."

We follow her into the kitchen where Piper, Molly, Carson, Kate, and Kenzi are happily playing with neon-green slime on plastic trays.

"Mommy!" Piper squeals, holding up her goo-covered hands. "Wanna play?"

I grimace. "Absolutely not. I am not a slime mom."

Madison grins. "That's okay. You're a baking mom and a park mom. I can be the slime mom."

"And I will happily outsource that," I laugh just as a knock sounds at the door.

"That's probably Carson's dad," Madison calls. "Can one of you let him in?"

"I got it," I volunteer, maybe a little too fast.

Madison smirks, making Andrew raise a brow, but I ignore both of them and head for the door.

I peek through the peephole and there he is, Eric. And wow, he somehow manages to look good just standing on a porch in a hoodie.

"Hey," he says with a smile that sends a little jolt through me. "Didn't expect to see you here."

"Sorry to disappoint."

He laughs. "Definitely not disappointed. This is a nice surprise."

Good grief. Flirting should be illegal when he looks like that.

"Our kids are in the kitchen, covered in slime," I warn him.

"On purpose?"

"Yes. And somehow, we still love Madison despite exposing our children to these types of activities."

When we make it back to the kitchen, Madison already has our kids cleaned up and is wrangling slime trays.

"Need help?" I ask.

"Nope. We'll probably play a bit longer before I clean up," she says with a shrug.

"Okay, we will leave you to it then. See you later." I shrug, leading Piper, Eric and Carson towards the living room.

"Daddy, can I go over to Piper's and play Minecraft?" Carson asks hopefully as he pauses to pick up his backpack.

"Carson," Eric says gently, "you can't just invite yourself over. I'm sure Ava and Piper have plans."

"Sorry, buddy. Not tonight," I say with a smile down at Carson. "But maybe we can plan a playdate soon."

"Like tomorrow?" Carson asks.

"Maybe this weekend?" I offer, glancing at Eric.

"We're free," he says with a nod.

"Perfect. Text me and we'll set it up."

Carson beams. "Yes! Piper, we can work on my Minecraft

house!"

"And eat nachos," Piper adds.

"Nachos sound perfect," Eric says. "Should I bring margaritas?"

My brows lift. "Only if you're willing to share."

"Always," he says with a grin that feels like it has a little extra meaning.

"Can we have margaritas?" Piper asks.

"You can have kid margaritas," I say.

"Deal," Piper shrugs, already halfway to the house.

Eric calls as he and Carson head for the car. "See you later, Ava."

"Bye, Eric. Bye, Carson."

On the porch, Piper turns and squints at me. "Do you have a crush on Carson's dad?"

"Maybe. Is that okay with you?"

She grins. "That's okay. Carson's nice. He always lets me be in charge."

"Well, I guess that means we should hang out with them more."

"Yep!" she says, skipping inside after I open the door.

Thank goodness, because I have a feeling our weekends are about to get a lot more fun.

* * *

"Happy closing day!" I greet Emilee and Adam in front of the closing company. "You guys excited?"

"Excited. Nervous. Anxious." Emilee admits.

"Well, the hard part is already over. Inspections are done.

97

Final walk through is complete. Funds have arrived. All you have to do is sign your life away today."

"Perfect. Easy peasy," Emilee says, forcing an uneasy smile. "Sorry, this is such a huge step but I'm so thankful for you helping us all along the way. We wouldn't have even considered buying a house if you hadn't encouraged us."

"And we would be making a house payment for some landlord instead of earning our own equity," Adam adds. "Really, we can't thank you enough for the help."

I grin. "Listen, that's all the thanks I need. I love being able to help people buy homes. Especially their first home."

"Well, even still we'd love to have you over for a little housewarming party once we are all settled in," Emilee says. "Piper, too of course."

"We'd love to come." I tell her with a smile, opening the door to the title office. "But right now we need to head inside and get this closing done. You have a lot of unpacking and moving to do today," I say before leading them into the building. We step into the lobby and take a seat.

As we get settled, Adam speaks up. "Speaking of having a lot to do today. Are there any moving companies around here? We have a storage unit full of heavy furniture and…"

"And Adam won't let me help." Emilee interrupts her husband, with a playful pat on his leg.

Adam raises a brow. "You're carrying our baby. That's enough heavy lifting. Besides, I don't mind paying someone to help us. It'll be a quick job if we have two or three guys pitch in."

"We don't have a moving company here in town, but in the past I've just posted on Facebook and usually have no problem finding at least a couple of teenage boys that can help. Want me to do that?" I offer.

"Yes. That'll be great." Emilee responds.

Without hesitation, I pick up my phone and make the post. "Done. Most everyone I can think of is at school until 3:30 so it may take a little while to get some help lined up."

"That's fine," Emilee assures me. "We can handle the boxes and the smaller stuff on our own while we wait."

"Ava, are you guys ready?" Jenna, the closing officer asks as she leans through the doorway into the lobby.

"Yes! Let's go buy a house."

* * *

"Gah! What a nightmare." I groan, staring down at my phone as I stand on the sidewalk in front of TBR.

"What's wrong?"

The deep voice makes me jump. I glance up to see Eric standing a few feet away, hand truck balanced in front of him, brown UPS cap shading his eyes. He looks annoyingly good for someone caught in the middle of a workday.

"Hey," I say, pushing a hand through my hair. "Today is just not working out the way it should."

His brows lift. "What happened?"

"Piper's aunt and uncle just closed on their house. Closing went great, but now they need help moving all their heavy furniture. She's pregnant, so she can't lift anything." I wave my phone in frustration. "Normally I can round up Madison's brother, Nathan, and a couple of his friends, but they have an away football game tonight. Basically the entire teenage boy population of Fawn Creek will be out of town until who knows when."

Eric leans against the hand truck, listening patiently. I cross my arms and sigh.

"I think I'm out of options. I mean, I could help, but I'm not exactly built for hauling dressers and sofas."

He doesn't even blink. "What time do they need help?"

I blink back at him. "I don't think they're picky. They'd just like to sleep in their new house tonight if they can. Why? Do you know someone?"

"Yeah." His mouth tips into a grin. "Me."

I stare at him. "You don't have to offer to help someone you've never even met move into their new house."

"I know I don't have to," he says easily, "but I don't mind. I don't have anything going on tonight. I'll probably be back in town around six, maybe a little earlier."

The relief that washes through me is ridiculous. "Really? If you're sure you don't mind, I'll let them know. They'll absolutely pay you for your time."

He waves me off. "They don't have to pay me. Seriously, I don't mind helping."

"Helping with what?"

We both turn to see Derek heading toward us, his uniform crisp, radio crackling faintly at his shoulder.

"Hey," Eric calls. "You busy tonight?"

Derek narrows his eyes. "Before I answer that question... why?"

Eric grins. "Care to help me help some strangers move into their new house? The wife's pregnant and can't lift anything heavy."

Derek looks between the two of us. "And how did you get roped into this?"

Eric jerks his thumb in my direction. "Her kid's aunt."

Recognition sparks, and Derek smirks. "Oh yeah, Avery told me you two were boinking or whatever."

My mouth falls open. "Um... we are not boinking."

"Okay, Ava. Whatever you say." He shrugs like he doesn't believe me for a second. "Anyway, just shoot me a text, Eric, and I'll come help. I'm off at four."

Before I can reply, Derek's radio crackles to life.

"Hey, Derek. You busy?" the dispatcher's voice asks.

Derek presses the talk button. "Nope, what's up?"

"Do you mind running by 611 Maple Street?"

"Yeah, sure. What's going on?"

"It's Mrs. McGlathery. She has a pickle jar she can't get open."

I slap a hand over my mouth to keep from laughing. Eric doesn't even try. He lets out a full laugh that causes me to do the same.

Derek groans. "Sure, I'll head that way now." He releases the button and gives us both a look. "This wasn't what I had in mind when I signed up to protect and serve my community. But, hey, it beats chasing criminals."

"Keeping Fawn Creek safe, one pickle jar at a time," I say. "See you later, Derek."

* * *

"Are you guys sure I can't pay you for your time?" Adam asks as he rolls the back of the U-Haul closed with a satisfying clang and turns to face Eric and Derek.

Derek waves him off with an easy grin. "No way. That took

101

less than half an hour. Besides, if you tried to pay me for moving furniture, my mom would probably ground me. I am going to head home, though. Long day."

Emilee steps out onto the porch, brushing her hands off on her jeans. "We have pizza and beer!" she calls out. "Isn't that the universal 'thanks for helping me move' payment?"

Eric chuckles, the sound low and warm. "Tempting, but I think Carson's about two minutes away from falling asleep standing up. I should probably get him home before he tips over."

"I know that feeling," I say with a laugh, tucking a stray hair behind my ear. "Tomorrow's going to be a busy day." I turn toward the yard. "Piper! Time to head home!"

"Carson, you too!" Eric calls, glancing toward where the kids are crouched over the grass with flashlights, still fascinated by whatever bug they've discovered.

Adam gives another grateful smile, looking a little more relaxed now that the last box is off the truck. "Seriously, thank you both again for everything. I don't know what we would've done without you."

I step closer to Emilee, heart tugging as I take in her tired but happy face. "I'm so glad we were able to get you fixed up," I tell her, wrapping her in a tight hug.

"You guys are lifesavers. Thank you so much." Emilee replies.

"That's just what small towns do. We take care of each other." I remind her.

Her arms tighten around me. "I'm so glad to be back," she says into my hair, voice soft and full. When we pull back, she smiles at me, eyes shiny but happy. "It's good to be home."

Chapter 14

"Hey!" I say to Mrs. Blum as I enter her classroom, dragging my wagon full of supplies behind me. It's Halloween. And not only do we have a busy night full of trick-or-treating, we also have a cram-packed school day. Fawn Creek Elementary has a tradition where the kids dress up in their costumes and then walk downtown to put on a parade. This allows everyone in town to see their costumes. After that, they walk back to the school, and each classroom has a Halloween party.

"Thank you so much for agreeing to be homeroom mom," the teacher says with a soft smile. "I know it's a big job, but we appreciate you so much."

I wave her off. "It's no problem. I've been waiting for this kind of stuff my whole life. I started making Pinterest boards for classroom parties when she was two."

Mrs. Blum lets out a laugh. "Well, we are lucky to have you then. If you want to get settled, I'll have the kids start getting ready for the parade. Some might need help with costumes or makeup. I had a few parents message me this morning, but so far it doesn't seem like it'll be anything too crazy."

"Oh, that's good, because Piper's costume is probably crazy enough for everyone," I admit with a laugh.

* * *

"Wait for me! I have little legs!" Piper calls out after us as we make our way out of the front door of the grade school wearing her inflatable pink axolotl costume.

"Girl, you're going to have to hustle a little bit," I tell her. "I know that costume is probably hard to walk in, but I warned you it wouldn't be easy."

"It's fine!" Piper calls out. "This fan actually makes it feel pretty good in here. I just have to figure out how to walk with my big tail and chunky legs."

I can't help but giggle as she speeds up to walk in front of me, her tail flailing from side to side. It's going to be a long night, but I love seeing my kid be so authentically herself.

We finish the short walk toward downtown, and the kids line up in preparation to start the parade.

"Hey. I'm going to go find Grandma, and then I'll walk back with you guys for the party."

"Okay!" Piper calls back through her costume, waving her arms in the air like a real-life cartoon character, causing an eruption of giggles from her classmates.

With Piper secured, I make my way down Main Street, watching for my parents. It doesn't take long to find them standing in front of TBR.

"Hey!" I greet them with a smile.

Weather for Halloween in Kansas is super unpredictable. One year it might be thirty degrees, another year it might be eighty-seven. But this year, we are lucky: it's a nearly perfect seventy degrees. Hopefully, this means we won't need coats with our costumes tonight.

"You look cute," Mom says, trying to read my shirt.

I pose, allowing her to see the full front. It's a black long-sleeve shirt with a haunted house that says: *Buying a house without a Realtor? Now that's spooky.* My business name and website are listed on the back, so I turn to show her that, too.

Mom laughs. "Okay, I love that."

"Thanks! Avery made it for me," I tell her. "She's been making all kinds of shirts for her mobile boutique and doing custom stuff here and there. I've been keeping her busy with all of my silly ideas. Before long, I'll have a wardrobe full of Fawn Creek Realty shirts."

"Well, tell her to make me one, please," Mom says.

"Me too," Dad adds, fiddling with the giant lens on the camera around his neck. "And see if she'll make me a hat, too."

"You'd really wear hats and shirts with my business on them?" I ask, raising a brow.

"Of course we would," Mom says without hesitation. "We're proud of you, Ava. You're building something special, and we love getting to cheer you on."

"Thanks, Mom."

Dad sets a hand on my shoulder. "We mean it. Most people don't accomplish half of what you have by thirty. You didn't let being a teen mom stop you. You turned it into something that made you stronger. Better. We're proud of you. Don't forget that."

The back of my throat tightens, but I manage a small nod. "I'll try not to."

"Hey."

I glance up to see Eric walking toward us, hand casually shoved in his pocket, looking infuriatingly good in his brown

UPS uniform.

"Just in time," he says, nodding toward the street where the kids are rounding the corner.

"Perfect timing," I agree, my stomach doing a weird little flip. My parents are standing right here, and this suddenly feels like a moment.

I turn to them. "Mom, Dad... this is my... friend... Eric. His son, Carson, goes to daycare with Piper."

Eric gives them both a polite smile and a small wave. "Nice to meet you."

My dad reaches forward and shakes his hand. "Nice to meet you. Is Carson in the parade, too?"

"Oh yes," Eric says. "He's a Minecraft Creeper this year and will be walking with the preschool class."

"That's one of those big, green, blocky characters." I chime in, gesturing with my hands.

"Oh, we know about Minecraft," Mom laughs.

"Piper's been giving us lessons," Dad adds, making Eric chuckle.

"Of course she has," I say with a laugh just as the preschool class makes its way toward us.

"Hey, is that Carson?" I ask, pointing to the green blocky kid walking at the front of the crowd.

"Yep, that's him," Eric says, pulling out his phone while Dad gets into position with his camera.

"Hey, buddy!" Eric calls.

"Daddy!" Carson squeals, jumping up and down in his blocky mask and green polyester suit.

"He's so cute," I say, smiling at Eric. "You headed back to work now?"

"In a second. I want to see Piper first."

"She should be up here any minute. Her costume is amazing. I just hope the batteries don't die before we get back to school."

"Batteries? What kind of costume needs batteries?" Dad asks, wrinkling his nose.

I point down the street at the pink axolotl inflatable bobbing toward us. "That kind."

"The pink thing?"

"That's her," I confirm.

"What is she supposed to be?" Mom asks.

"An axolotl."

"An axo-what?" Dad asks, leaning forward.

"It's an aquatic salamander," I explain. "She and basically every kid on the planet are obsessed with them."

"So it's a Minecraft thing, too?" Mom asks.

"Nope, they're real. She wants one for a pet, but I'm not sure I'm ready for the whole feeding-it-worms thing."

"Maybe Grandma and Grandpa will get her one," Mom teases.

"Will you come over every day to feed it worms?" I shoot back, grinning. "Let's wait until she's old enough to do it herself."

"Fine," Mom grumbles, but she's smiling.

"Hi, Piper!" I call as she approaches. She stops to wave, posing with her arms and stubby air-filled legs spread wide.

"She's such a cool kid," I say, laughing.

"She gets it from her mom," Eric says with a wink.

Before I can reply, he leans down and, without thinking, presses a quick kiss to my lips.

In front of my parents.

In front of the entire town of Fawn Creek.

In front of my daughter, who immediately turns to check if

107

I'm walking back to school with her.

My cheeks burn.

"Well." I clear my throat, half-laughing. "That's one way to hard-launch a new relationship. Surprise, everyone!"

* * *

Madison: So... did everyone see that?

Tyler: YEP.

Sierra: Absolutely.

Avery: See what?

Ava: Yeah... see what?

Our group chat is blowing up, and while I know exactly what Madison means, I'm hoping I'm wrong. Leaving the chat open, I speed-walk to catch up with Piper's class on their way back to the school.

Madison: Oh, just Ava hard-launching her new relationship with Eric... right in the middle of Main Street, in front of the entire town.

Avery: Aw, crap. I always miss the good stuff. What happened?

Madison: She was making out with Eric.

Ava (typing furiously): I was not making out with Eric. It was a peck. And I don't think he even meant to.

Tyler: Looked like he meant to do it from where I was standing.

Sierra: Agreed. No hesitation.

Avery: So... are you guys officially official now?

Ava: Honestly? I have no idea. I guess that's a conversation I have to have with him. How does one even do this stuff at our age? Do I ask him if he wants to go steady or... what?

Madison: I think you just ask if he wants to be exclusive. But, uh... he kissed you in front of your parents. I think you already have your answer.

Why am I freaking out right now? My heart's racing, my cheeks are hot, and I feel like half the town is watching me through this chat.

* * *

"Alright, guys, are we ready to go?" Andrew calls through the sliding rear window of his truck. Tyler's riding shotgun, and Molly's strapped into her car seat behind him. Madison, Kate, Kenzi, Avery, Derek, Juliet, Piper, and I are perched on hay bales lining the trailer, bundled in blankets as Andrew gets ready to chauffeur us through Fawn Creek for our night of trick-or-treating.

"Ready!" we all call back just as a voice rings out from down the street.

"Hey, wait!"

We turn to see Sierra and Cody heading our way, coffee cups in one hand and blankets in the other.

"You almost forgot us!" Sierra laughs.

"I didn't know you guys wanted to hang out with all of us on Halloween," Andrew says, shrugging.

"And miss the chance for cotton candy and funnel cake? Absolutely not," Sierra says. "Just because we don't have kids doesn't mean we aren't a couple of kids ourselves. Now, scoot over."

Once they climb aboard and get settled, Andrew eases the truck forward, the trailer creaking as we roll toward the residential streets of Fawn Creek.

"So, what's the game plan?" someone asks over the sound of gravel crunching under the tires.

"To get candy!" Kate shouts, holding up the wooden baseball bat that completes her *A League of Their Own* costume.

"And funnel cake!" Kenzi adds, fluffing her sparkly princess dress. Her costume couldn't be more different from her sister's, and I love that about them.

Madison shakes her head, smiling. "West side of town first, then we'll cross the highway and hit the east side, ending with Nightmare on Bradley and funnel cakes. And then we'll be in bed by 9:30. Hopefully."

"Hey." Avery nudges my leg. "Is that Eric and Carson?"

I look across the street and spot them immediately. Eric's helping Carson adjust his creeper mask. I lift my hand to wave. "That's them."

"Want to see if they want to come with us?" Avery teases, wiggling her eyebrows.

"Sure," I say, trying to sound casual. "Halloween in Fawn Creek is a lot more fun with a group. Andrew, can you stop one more time?"

Andrew groans but pulls the truck to the curb anyway. Cody leans over the side of the trailer and calls out, "Hey, Eric! Wanna join us?"

Eric glances down at Carson, then back at us. "Do you have room?"

"We'll make room," I say with a grin. "Come on up."

* * *

"Okay, let's get a few pictures while we're waiting in line for funnel cake," Avery says, her phone already in hand. She points toward the photo backdrop in front of the house, nestled between two giant inflatables. "Tyler, Andrew... get over there."

Andrew and Tyler move into place first, laughing as they try to look serious for the camera. Molly waddles after them in the tiniest Beauty and the Beast gown, the skirt puffing around her like a yellow cloud. Avery snaps the photo and coos over how cute she looks.

Next up are Avery, Derek, and Juliet. Juliet's been obsessed with *Pinkalicious* lately. Probably thanks to Tyler and the stack of books she keeps buying her. So, it's no surprise when she twirls in front of the camera in her pink dress and glittery crown.

"Okay, Ava, your turn," Avery calls.

Piper and I step up to the backdrop, both of us smiling at the camera. Eric stands a few feet away with Carson, watching.

"Do you want to get in here with us?" I ask.

"Okay!" Carson blurts out before Eric can answer, running to stand beside Piper.

Eric laughs and joins us, standing close enough that his arm brushes mine. He reaches down to squeeze my hand, just like he did on the hayride. The familiar warmth of it makes my stomach flutter.

"Let's get one of just you two," I tell him, gesturing toward Carson. "Then we'll grab a group shot with all the kids."

A few more flashes, a handful of smiles, and we're done just in time to reach the front of the line. The smell of powdered sugar fills the air, mixing with the chill of October. The Nightmare on Bradley never disappoints. It's a full-blown Halloween wonderland. Giant spider webs stretch across the yard, inflatables tower over the crowd, and strings of orange lights flicker against the trees. At the end of the maze, the prize: a plate of warm mini funnel cakes dusted in sugar.

I'm not sure who's more excited, the kids or us, but everyone agrees it's the best stop of the night.

With our sugary treats in hand, we make our way back toward the trailer, the kids chattering between bites.

"Thanks for letting us tag along tonight," Eric says beside me.

"Of course. I'm glad you came." I glance up at him. "What's your plan for the rest of the night?"

He shakes his head. "This is it for me."

"Would you and Carson like to come over and hang out? Maybe turn on a movie for the kids?" I ask, biting my lip. For some reason, this guy makes me braver than I've ever been. Making a move doesn't scare me at all. I actually like it.

Eric looks down at Carson and smiles. "I bet he'd like that. And I would too."

* * *

"Okay, guys, we'll be out on the porch if you need us," I tell Piper and Carson, tucking the blanket around them before they settle in with their movie.

Eric grabs the bowl of candy from the table by the door, and I follow him outside. The porch swing creaks softly as we sit, the candy bowl resting on the small table beside us.

"I don't know if we'll get any more trick-or-treaters, but

it's worth a shot," I say with a shrug. "I love living in a neighborhood where kids actually come to the door."

Eric nods, his voice quiet and thoughtful. "It is nice. My parents live just outside of town, so we never got anyone. They ended up putting a trailer on their property for me and Carson, so he's never really known a true Fawn Creek Halloween until now."

"I hope he loved it."

Eric smiles and slides his hand into mine. "Oh, he did. So did I."

For a moment, the only sound is the faint chatter from the TV inside and the rustle of leaves across the porch. I glance down at our joined hands, then back at him. "So... about that kiss downtown at the parade."

"Yeah," he says, running a hand through his hair. "I'm sorry. I didn't think it through, with your parents not knowing about us. Kissing you goodbye just felt natural. I didn't give it a second thought."

I shake my head. "It's okay. I didn't mind. I guess the whole town's going to find out eventually anyway." I look back down at our hands again, my stomach fluttering. "So... does that mean we're dating?"

Eric's lips curve into a smirk. "Well, you're the only person I want to be kissing. Do you want to be kissing anyone else?"

I shake my head. "Nope. Can't say that I do."

"So that settles it. We're only kissing each other."

"Yes, agreed. And that means you're my boyfriend? Or are you too cool for labels?" I tease, nudging him lightly with my elbow.

"Ava, label me however you want," he says with a grin. "Yes, I'm your boyfriend, and I'm going to kiss you now."

"I don't know what took you so long," I laugh as he leans in. His lips meet mine, soft at first, then deeper, until—

"Ewwww!"

"Why are they kissing?!"

"Do you have any candy?"

We break apart and look toward the sidewalk where three teenage boys stand, one holding up a plastic grocery bag.

"Umm... trick or treat?" I manage, trying not to laugh.

Chapter 15

"Ava! Thanks so much for coming by!" Emilee says, swinging open the front door to welcome us into her housewarming party.

"Thanks for inviting us," I say as she pulls me into a hug. "This place looks so good already." I look around the house. "It took no time for you guys to get settled and make it feel like home."

"We have a lot of updating we'd like to do," she admits. "Walls to paint, carpet to replace, and so on, but this is great for now."

"Well, it already looks so good. I'm sure when you put your creative touch on it, it will really shine."

"Thank you. Hey Piper, Jacob is out back playing on his swing set if you want to go out there," Emilee tells my daughter. "You can go through the kitchen."

"Bye, Mom!" Piper exclaims, sprinting through Emilee's house as though she owns the place.

"Sorry about my kid. She has no problem making herself at home no matter where she is," I tell Emilee, shaking my head.

"Girl, she is 100 percent my brother's kid. You do not have to apologize. In fact, my parents should be apologizing to you," she says, leading me into the kitchen.

"Apologizing for what?" asks Susanne, standing at the counter arranging a tray of pinwheels.

Emilee walks over and plucks a pinwheel off the top of the pile. "For Piper being just like Zach."

Susanne frowns. "Piper is perfect. There is nothing to apologize for."

"I just mean she has Zach's personality."

"And?" her mother challenges. "He was a free spirit. I loved that about him."

Emilee shakes her head. "Free spirit is just a label parents give their kids to excuse them for being little assholes. Don't get me wrong. Zach grew up to be a great guy, but he was a pain when we were kids."

Susanne scoffs. "Emilee, you can't just talk about your brother like that. He's not here to defend himself. Besides, are you calling Piper a pain?"

Emilee shakes her head. "No. I love Piper. She has all the best parts of Zach. She's fun and funny, outspoken and far from shy. She's her own person, and I love that. Luckily, she is part Ava too, and that keeps her from being a pain like he was."

I shake my head and chuckle. "I heard stories about when he was a kid. Jumping off the roof with a trash bag as a parachute, taking apart the toaster to see how it worked... thankfully Piper got just enough caution from me to keep her safe. I see a lot of him in her. It's nice to catch glimpses of him every once in a while."

Susanne nods. "Jacob is more like Emilee as a kid. Soft-spoken, able to play alone without too much complaining. I'm curious what the next baby will be like."

Emilee shrugs. "I suppose if baby number two is just like my brother, it wouldn't be the worst thing ever."

* * *

"That was so fun!" Piper exclaims, skipping a few steps ahead on the sidewalk. "I'm so glad Aunt Emilee and Jacob moved here."

I glance down at her wide grin and can't help but smile. Me too, baby. "Me too."

"Grandma said maybe I can come to Thanksgiving at their house this year. Is that okay?"

"Yep," I say. "They're doing Thanksgiving lunch, so you'll go over there. Then I'll pick you up and take you to your other grandma's for dinner."

"I'm going to eat so much pie that day," she predicts, already licking her lips. "I can't wait."

"Oh, I know you will," I laugh. "Maybe you and I can work on making a pie for you to take to Grandma's for Thanksgiving. It's good manners to bring something when you show up at someone else's house to eat."

"Oh! Can we make a pumpkin pie?" she asks. "Maybe we can get a pumpkin from the store and empty out its guts and bake it in the oven."

I grimace. "How about we just get a can of pumpkin from the store and make it that way?" I suggest. "I'm a decent cook, but I'm not sure I could make a good pumpkin-gut pie."

Piper groans. "Fine."

"But you can help me. And I'll teach you how to make pie crust."

"Okay!" Piper perks up immediately as she begins to skip ahead of me.

I pull my phone from my jacket pocket and fire off a text to

Eric.

Ava: I survived the housewarming party.

Immediately, I see the notification on my screen that he's read the message, and three dots appear, telling me that he's typing a response.

Eric: Glad to hear it. I was about to send a search party. Did you have a good time?

Ava: Actually, yeah. It was great. I barely got Piper out of there. I had to bribe her with promises of going home to make s'mores on the fire pit. Do you guys want to come join us?

I watch Piper making her way toward the house, unaware of my phone conversation. My chest warms at the thought of Eric and Carson showing up for a casual evening.

Eric: Absolutely. Need me to bring anything?

Ava: Just yourselves. See you around seven?

Eric: We'll be there.

I slide my phone back into my pocket and smile at Piper, who's already running ahead to open the door. The evening air feels crisp, and the sky is turning that soft twilight blue. It's the best time of the year.

I take a deep breath and follow her inside, ready to start the cozy night of s'mores and laughter.

* * *

"Okay, Piper. How do you like your marshmallow?" Eric asks from his crouched position right outside the fire pit.

"Burnt," she answers.

"Burnt?"

"Burnt," I confirm. "Like, just to the point where it doesn't appear to be edible, but right before it falls off the stick and into the fire. That's the sweet spot."

Eric smirks. "Sounds complicated."

I hug my knees where I'm sitting next to Piper. "Many marshmallows have met their demise while I've learned to perfect the art of the perfect Piper marshmallow toastiness. Don't beat yourself up if you can't manage to accomplish it on your first try."

"Well, I'm not one to step down from a challenge," he informs me with a flirtatious wink that causes my heart to flip. After a few moments of Eric concentrating on getting her marshmallow just right, he removes the stick from the flames and turns towards my daughter. "Piper, how's this look?" He holds up the marshmallow in question.

"Not bad."

He chuckles. "Glad you approve." He slides the marshmallow off the stick and assembles her s'more. Then he presents her with a paper plate containing the finished product. "Your dessert, ma'am."

"Thank you," Piper grins in response before furrowing her brow and pointing at his bicep. "Hey, what's that on your arm?"

Eric takes a seat on the ground next to her before pushing up his sleeve the rest of the way. "It's a tattoo. It's Carson's footprint from when he was a baby."

Piper frowns. "Did your mom get mad that you drew on

yourself?"

Eric laughs, the sound warm and unguarded. "No, she actually came with me when I got it done."

I can't help but glance at the small footprint inked into his skin. There's something about the way he's smiling. He looks so proud, and a little nostalgic. It makes my chest ache in the sweetest way.

Piper turns to me with a tiny bit of melted marshmallow stuck to her chin. "Mom, do you have any tattoos?"

I shake my head. "No, I sure don't."

"Because your mom said no?" she asks knowingly.

I can't help but chuckle. "No, I just don't like needles, and they use needles to give you a tattoo."

"Needles?!" Carson exclaims. "Daddy, I don't like needles. Do I have to get a tattoo when I get big?"

"No, kiddo. You do not have to get a tattoo if you don't want one," Eric assures him.

"I'm gonna get one," Piper informs us. "Mom, can I get a tattoo tomorrow?"

I cock my head to the side and look at my daughter. "What would you want a tattoo of?"

"A unicorn, duh."

I shake my head. "Sorry kid, no tattoos until you're 18."

"Fine," she groans. "Can I have another s'more instead?"

"Sure," I answer, moving to pick up the stick.

Piper shakes her head. "I want Eric to make it. He makes the best s'mores."

Eric grins and reaches for another marshmallow. "High praise coming from a professional marshmallow critic. Guess I'd better live up to my reputation."

I catch his eye across the firelight, and for a second it feels like there's more than just smoke making my chest feel warm.

Chapter 16

"Hey, come on in," Sierra says, holding open Tyler's front door for me, Piper, Carson, and Eric. "You can put your food down on the kitchen counter. Everyone else is out on the back patio."

We drop off our pies and macaroni and cheese and make our way out the back door to join our friends.

"Happy Friendsgiving!" Tyler announces cheerily. "I'm so glad you could make it."

It's the weekend before Thanksgiving. Tyler had the idea to gather everyone for a Friendsgiving at her house. Instead of traditional food, the boys are smoking ribs, and everyone else was asked to bring sides.

"Thanks for the invite," I say with a smile. "Your house is beautiful."

"We are just glad to finally have it done," Andrew says, wrapping an arm around Tyler's waist. "It feels like it took years to get everything the way we wanted it."

"Well, it was worth the wait," I tell him. "I think it's so cool that you get to have your brother and sister-in-law right next door."

"It's actually as great as you'd think," Tyler confesses. "Sometimes, we meet up on the porch for a beer after Molly goes to bed. Or if I run out of something, I can run next door and borrow it without going into town."

Sierra shrugs. "Heck, I've stolen milk from their fridge without them knowing."

Tyler deadpans. "Seriously? I thought I was losing my mind when I came home one night. I swore I had a full half-gallon of milk in the morning, and by night, the seal was broken and just a little missing. Andrew doesn't drink milk."

"Nope," Sierra confesses. "Just a cocoa pebble emergency. I carried my bowl right over and got some. I've also stolen a stick of butter before."

"We need cameras," Tyler says to Andrew.

"I'll just wave at them as I walk by," Sierra shrugs.

"I swear some days I think you two are the ones that are related, not Cody and Andrew," Madison laughs.

"I've known her since I was little. She's my big sister whether she likes it or not," Sierra laughs.

"The marriage just made it official," Tyler adds.

"Are you guys done bickering and ready to eat?" Cody asks, opening the lid to the smoker. "Ribs are done."

Inside, we line up to fill our plates. Our friend group has grown enough that we overflow from the dining room table onto two folding tables.

Tyler takes a seat, pulling Molly's high chair up next to her, and pauses with a soft smile, as though lost in the moment.

"You okay, babe?" Andrew asks, reaching up to squeeze her hand.

She nods. "Yeah. I was just thinking about how lucky we all are. A few years ago, I didn't know half of you. Now, we're married, we have this house, I have my bookstore, you have your construction company, and we have Molly. Not to mention that we have so many friends we need folding tables for dinner.

I love this. I love all of you, and I'm just so glad life brought us together."

"Well, I propose a toast," Avery says, holding up her red solo cup. "May we have many more Friendsgivings together, and may we find at least one more table before next year since our group keeps growing."

Madison turns to Avery. "Does that mean you have something to tell us?"

Derek grins. "There's a reason she skipped out on Tyler's margaritas tonight."

My jaw drops. "Seriously? Are you having a baby?"

Avery pulls out her phone and holds it up to show us a photo of an ultrasound. "Actually, there's two."

"Two?!" Bryan exclaims, nearly choking on his beer. "So, I'm getting two more nieces or nephews?"

"It looks like it," Avery shrugs. "Mom doesn't know yet, but I'll tell her Thursday at Thanksgiving lunch."

"Man, I thought no one could top the Christmas when I told her I was moving back, but you found a way," Bryan chuckles. "Congrats, sis."

"Derek, are you okay?" I ask.

He nods. "Scared to death, but we're excited."

Tyler takes a sip of her margarita and shakes her head. "We are definitely going to need a bigger table next year."

* * *

"Now that was a great Thanksgiving dinner," Eric says as we get into the car.

I nod. "Our group definitely keeps things fun."

"I like them. Everyone made me and Carson feel like we've been a part of things for years."

"They are good at that," I say, squeezing his hand. "Hey, speaking of which, we are taking a group beach trip to Georgia in January. We are renting a house on Tybee Island, and I'm the only one without a roommate. You want to join me?"

"Are you asking me to bunk with you at the beach?" Eric teases, "because yes, I'd love to."

"I was hoping you'd say that. We're splitting the cost of the house between each couple. My portion is already paid, so all you have to worry about is your airplane ticket."

"I would love to. Send me the dates, and I'll make sure I can get off work," he says.

I grin as I settle back against the seat, a giddy flutter rising in my stomach. Beach trip secured.

* * *

The next few days pass in a blur of school drop-offs, work, and last-minute grocery store runs. Before I know it, Thanksgiving is here.

"Hello!" I call into my parents' house as I step inside. The smells of turkey, pies, and all the fixings waft through the house, making my stomach rumble. It smells just like home.

"In the kitchen!" Mom calls back. "Come on in!"

I slide a tray of deviled eggs onto the island.

"Those look amazing," Mom says. "But I told you didn't have to bring anything."

"I know, but I like to cook, and Piper loves deviled eggs."

"And you can never have too many deviled eggs for Thanksgiving," Dad adds, sneaking one from the tray. "Oh, these are good."

"Piper, you can go play with your cousins in the living room. Dinner will be ready in ten minutes," Mom tells her.

"Okay, Gram," Piper says, heading to the living room just as my sister-in-law, Tosha, steps in.

"Hey, I thought I heard you," she says, pulling me into a hug. "How are you?"

"I'm good. I've missed you guys. It's not fair we only see you a couple times a year."

"I know. I wish Caleb had more time off so we could come more often. Maybe you and Piper should come to Denver for a weekend."

"That would be so much fun. I'll check my schedule."

"Mom said you're seeing someone," Tosha adds with a raised brow. "You could always invite him along, too."

I turn to look at my mom. "Mother." I scold her. "Are you spreading this news to everyone or just our immediate family?"

"What?" she asks, looking offended. "I thought everyone already knew."

I sigh. "I mean, it's not a secret or anything. You know how this town is. I just try to keep my private life... private."

Tosha raises an eyebrow. "Ava, I'm your sister. We should have no secrets. Do you have a picture? I need to see this guy."

I roll my eyes but pull out my phone and easily locate a picture of Eric in my photo album. Honestly, I'm excited to show him off. I mean, the man *is* beautiful. Swiping through the pictures, I show Tosha.

"He is cute! And is that his son? He's adorable too," Tosha gushes.

I beam proudly. "Yes! His name is Carson, and he is the sweetest kid ever. He is always giving out hugs and cuddles.

And he follows Piper around like she is the queen of the world."

Tosha laughs. "Well, she kind of is. Have you met her?"

"She's my boss, that's for sure." I agree.

"Is he going to Savannah with you?" Mom asks.

"Yes," I nod. "I just asked him the other night, and as long as we are still together by then, he is coming on our group trip."

"So, things are serious then?" Tosha asks, leaning against the counter as though I'm about to give her all the juicy details.

I pause to consider the question. "Well, we've been dating for about a month. Ever since right around Halloween. I really like him and his son."

Tosha smiles brightly. "That's great. What about the baby mama? Is she around?"

I shake my head. "No, she isn't. She decided when Carson was little that she didn't want to be a mom. She signed over her rights and took off."

Tosha sticks out her bottom lip. "That's so sad."

"I know. That kid is the sweetest. I can't imagine just deciding you don't want anything to do with him. Who does that?"

Tosha shakes her head. "A monster, obviously. But, yay for you because that means that you hopefully won't have to deal with some jealous ex popping up and causing issues."

"Hopefully you're right," I say, popping an olive in my mouth from the nearby veggie tray.

"Okay, guys, dinner is ready!" Mom announces. "Let's eat."

Chapter 17

"Hey!" I poke my head into Avery's mobile boutique.

It's the Saturday after Thanksgiving, and Fawn Creek is bustling with energy. Every year on Small Business Saturday, Fawn Creek puts on a tree-lighting ceremony in the evening. During the day, in addition to all of the stores running sales, there's a large craft fair at the Blackledge Event Center.

Vendors of all kinds fill the second and third floors of the building, while shoppers come from miles away to get a jump start on their Christmas shopping.

Recently, Avery and Derek remodeled an old travel trailer and transformed it into a mobile boutique. Today, the trailer is parked in downtown Fawn Creek, ready for its first big holiday season.

"It is so freaking festive in here," I swoon as I step onto the metal step and make my way inside, eyeing the white Christmas lights and pink tinsel adorning the inside of the camper. "You've been busy."

"Thanks!" Avery smiles proudly. "Busy is an understatement. I've been working constantly for months to get ready for the holiday season. I swear Christmas prep is a full-time job."

My eyes wander, admiring the racks of clothes and shelves of accessories that Avery has either made herself or gathered over the course of the last few months.

"And then add that on top of my actual full-time job, plus content creating, and then add being pregnant with twins. I'm exhausted."

"I'm exhausted just hearing you talk about it." I shake my head. "I still can't believe you're having twins. How are you going to balance everything with two babies? Are you going to keep working full time?"

She shakes her head. "I doubt it. I mean, Madison is a great daycare provider, and I know my babies will be safe with her, but I am pretty much convinced that this will be the tipping point for me to become a stay-at-home mom. As soon as I knew I was having Juliet, I knew I would want something that allowed me more time freedom so I could be available for her. I think this is my final push."

I nod. "Hey, it makes sense. You are already so busy with your content creation and now your boutique."

Avery nods. "Absolutely. I love my job, but I also know I'm going to want to be home with the babies. Especially with Derek's schedule."

"I don't think anyone would blame you," I tell her, as I browse a nearby table of earrings, holding up a pair of sparkly royal blue ones to examine closer. I immediately decide to purchase them. "You have to do what's right for your family."

"That's the plan. Ever since we found out, we have been doubling down to save as much money as possible to keep me from having to return to work. Between that and paying for the lawyer, of course."

I furrow my brows. "What lawyer? I missed something."

Avery puts her hand over her mouth. "Oh my gosh, I can't believe I didn't tell you. Juliet's dad wants to sign over his rights to Juliet. Derek is adopting her." Avery shakes her head. "I thought I posted that in the group chat, but now I'm seriously doubting it. Stupid pregnancy brain."

"Oh, I would have remembered that text for sure," I assure her. "Avery, that's amazing. I mean, I'm sad for Juliet that this is the case, but in the long run it'll be so much better for you to not deal with him."

Avery nods. "Yes, absolutely. He's been better for the last few months, thankfully. There for a while, he was determined to be a dad, but once he figured out that I didn't want anything to do with him romantically, he just decided to quit trying to force a relationship with Juliet. Now he doesn't even bother visiting her."

Just hearing about how Cory is dropping the ball when it comes to his daughter breaks my heart. But also, it doesn't really surprise me. He's never been a great guy. "Ugh. She's so lucky she has Derek. He loves her so much."

"And he's the best stepdad I could ask for," she agrees as she works to finish setting things up for the craft show to start. "Life really seems to be falling into place for us, for all of us, really."

"Yeah, it is," I agree, my mind already going to Eric and Carson and the fact that the four of us are slowly becoming a family unit too.

Avery smirks as though she's reading my mind. "I'm so glad you and Eric are seeing each other. And that he's coming to Georgia. You two are so good together," she gushes. "Oh my gosh, my hormones are insane. I think I'm going to start crying."

I let out a soft chuckle. "Hey, don't ruin your makeup. You are going to have a hard day selling clothes with mascara running down your face."

"Or they'll feel sorry for me and buy more," Avery laughs.

I hand over the handful of things I've chosen as we've been chatting. "Well, I'll take these. And they are not a pity purchase, I promise."

"Thanks, friend," she smiles.

* * *

After an afternoon of browsing the Christmas Market in the Blackledge Building, I drop my bags at home and head to Emilee's to pick up Piper. When Emilee offered to keep her so I could knock out some shopping today, I accepted immediately. Even before I knock, the familiar sound of *The Floor Is Lava* blares from the living room speakers.

Emilee greets me at the door, and I follow her inside, grinning at the scene before me. Piper is in full command of the living room, jumping from pillow to pillow, Jacob hot on her heels as the TV counts down their imaginary doom.

"Mommy!" Piper squeals when she spots me. "Jump! The floor is lava!"

Emilee and I exchange a look. With a resigned sigh, I start hopping in place, feet barely leaving the floor. Emilee gives a token bounce from one foot to the other.

"Mom! You have to jump," Jacob scolds.

"This is the best I can offer, kiddo," Emilee says with a shrug.

"Why? Because you're really old?" Jacob asks.

"No, it's because her baby might fall out of her butt," Piper explains matter-of-factly.

Jacob nods in total agreement. "Oh. Makes sense."

Emilee is doubled over laughing while I do my best to keep a straight face. "Is that one of those things I should correct," I whisper, "or do I do more damage by fixing it?"

"Leave it," Emilee gasps between laughs. "Comedy gold."

"Fair enough." The game ends, and I flop onto the couch next to Piper. "You guys coming to the tree-lighting festival tonight?" I ask Emilee.

"Oh, definitely. Jacob is pumped to see Santa," she says, still grinning. "And honestly, I'm excited for my first real Fawn Creek festival. I missed small-town stuff when we were in Overland Park. It just wasn't the same."

I nod. "I get it. A lot of people can't wait to leave their hometowns, but for me... this place is just home."

Emilee smiles softly.

"After Zach died, this town took care of me and Piper," I continue. "They didn't have to. I was a teen mom. They could have left it all to my parents. Instead, they started a savings account for Piper, dropped diapers and wipes on my porch, even added money to a grocery store tab. They gave us more than I ever expected, and I'll never stop being grateful. I've tried to make it my mission to give back as much as I can."

"They took great care of Mom and Dad, too." Emilee agrees. "A family friend raised money for the funeral, and we had more casseroles than our freezer could hold."

"Cooking is some people's love language," I say with a small smile. "It's how they process their own grief."

"Maybe," she says with a laugh, patting her belly. "Right now, cooking just feels like a chore."

"You're busy growing a whole human," I remind her. "You're doing exactly enough."

"Mommy, can we get hot chocolate tonight?" Piper pipes up,

bouncing onto my lap. "And see Santa?"

"Yes," I tell her, smoothing her hair. "Hot chocolate, Santa, and the big tree. We wouldn't miss it."

* * *

"Hi." I lean into the car and give Eric a quick kiss before Piper and I climb inside.

"Thanks for picking us up."

"You're welcome." He squeezes my hand as I buckle in. "Hey, Piper. Ready to see Santa?"

"Yes!" Piper shouts, her pigtails bouncing. "He has the best candy canes. I can't wait for one."

"Candy canes and Santa? Sounds like a great night. And don't forget they're lighting the big tree," Eric reminds her.

"I know! We made ornaments at school for the fire department to hang on it," Piper says proudly.

"Every kid at school did?" Eric asks.

"Yep."

"Even you, Carson?"

"Yeah," Carson pipes up from the backseat. "We even walked downtown and watched the firefighters put them up. They used a giant ladder."

Eric glances at him in the rearview mirror, one brow raised. "Wait, was this one of the days I asked if you did anything fun at school and you said 'no'?"

Carson just shrugs.

I laugh. "It happens. Last year, they duct-taped the principal to the wall during an assembly and threw whipped cream at him. Piper was one of the kids throwing it! I didn't find out until the school posted it on Facebook a week later."

Eric chuckles. "Why were they throwing whipped cream at the principal?"

"Something to do with reading points." I grin. "Piper didn't understand why I was so shocked she forgot to mention it. We never got to do anything like that when I was in school."

Eric shakes his head, grinning. "Man, I'd love to throw whipped cream at my boss."

"Maybe just wait until after he approves your vacation," I tease.

"Oh, he already did. Got the email this morning."

"Yay!" I squeeze his hand. "Well, you better still hold off on throwing things at him. We don't want to risk him changing his mind."

* * *

"Hello, little girl. What can I get you for Christmas this year?" Santa asks as Piper climbs into his lap.

Every year the Fawn Creek Fire Department supplies the Santa for the annual tree-lighting festival. A few years ago, Cody got the job. Unfortunately for him, he is just good enough at it that he has been stuck doing it ever since.

"Well, I've been thinking that I'd really like a pet," Piper says. "But not a basic pet. Something cool that everyone in town will be jealous of. Especially that meanie head Marina."

"Uh..." Santa says, buying time. "I don't think you can get on the nice list by calling someone a meanie head."

"Well, she started it. She told me that I look like a boy because my ears aren't pierced. Then she told me I'm not a good cheerleader and my hair is too straight." Piper shrugs. "I just want to make her a little jealous."

Santa turns to look at me and then back at Piper. "What kind of pet are we thinking?"

"I'm thinking a sea otter."

Santa blinks. "I don't think a sea otter would want to live in a house."

"We have a big garage and we don't even park our car in there most of the time. We could get him a tank to keep in there, and I could feed him a fish every day before school." Piper is completely serious. "It would be extra cool if you can make sure he stays baby-sized forever. Then I could pick him up every day and cuddle him. Maybe I could learn how to scuba dive and swim around in his tank with him."

Santa shakes his head. "I'm sorry, kiddo. I don't think owning a sea otter is legal in the city limits."

"Fine." Piper sighs dramatically. "Just get my mom a husband then."

My face heats instantly. Eric chokes on a laugh and tries to hide it with a cough.

Cody glances between us, then turns back to Piper. "I'll see what I can do about that sea otter."

"Thanks, Santa. Can I have a candy cane now?"

Cody hands her one and smirks at me. "Good luck, Mom."

"Thanks a lot, Santa. I can't wait to find her a sea otter," I mutter, shaking my head.

"You could always fall back on the other gift idea," Cody teases.

Chapter 18

"Hey, come on in," Madison says, leading me inside her house on the last day of daycare before Christmas Eve. "The kids and I are just wrapping up our Christmas party."

"Okay, no worries. I'm in no rush," I assure her. "You look super festive, by the way. Your shirt is perfect." I point to her shirt that says *Tree tops glisten and children listen... to nothing. Children literally don't listen to anything.*

"Oh, thank you! I saw a photo online and had to have Avery make it for me," she says, leading me into the kitchen where the kids are sitting at the table with plates of decorated Christmas cookies in front of them.

I hand Madison the red sparkly gift bag I carried inside. "Merry Christmas."

"Aww, thank you, Ava." Madison peeks inside the bag before carrying it to the counter.

"That's from me!" Piper says from her spot at the table with a freshly decorated cookie. She has remnants of green frosting across the bridge of her nose.

"It's from all of us," I correct her. "All the parents went in together this year."

Madison grins and pulls out the first item. "Oh, a candle. Cinnamon roll. I love it."

"My mom picked that one out at the Crafty Candle Shop," Piper announces. "It smells super yummy. Keep going!"

"Okay, okay. What else do we have here... oh, a shirt that says *Chaos Coordinator*. That is definitely me."

"Juliet's mom made it," Piper adds.

Madison continues pulling things from the bag. "And a gift card to Drip with a bag of fancy coffee."

"Because you drink a lot of coffee," Carson giggles.

"Well, you guys make me need a lot of coffee," Madison responds. "Oh, and there's a card." She opens it and pauses to read it. "With a gift card inside for Sierra's salon and a gift certificate for the bookstore. Plus, all of you signed the card," she gushes. "Thank you, guys. I love it and I feel so spoiled."

Madison makes her way around the dining room table, pausing to hug each child and thank them. "I'm going to miss you guys over Christmas Break."

"We'll miss you too," I tell her as we move toward the sink to clean up the dishes from the kids decorating their cookies. "But you deserve a break. It'll be good to just hang out with Bryan and the girls for a few days."

"I'm ready. I need sleep, and it'll be nice to catch up on wedding planning." She grins. "Are you and Eric doing anything together for the holidays?"

"We are planning to do something on Christmas Eve evening with the kids. We're thinking a movie, snacks, and making cookies. Then he'll go back to his house, and we will see each other after Christmas. We didn't want to drag the kids around more than they already will be."

"I think that's great," Madison says. "So you guys are getting serious then, if you're combining traditions?"

I shrug, smiling. "I guess so. I like him. A lot. He's a great dad, and he's so sweet to Piper."

"And not bad to look at either," Madison mutters in a teasing tone.

"That helps."

She lowers her voice. "So, how's the... you know?"

I raise a brow. "Actually, I don't know. We haven't gotten there yet."

"Sheesh. You're taking it slow," she says, gently scrubbing a plastic tray covered in green frosting.

I sigh. "What choice do we have? We always have the kids. There are no other parents to send them off with for the weekend. We never have alone time."

Madison shakes her head. "You have to fix that. Want me to keep the kids so you can do so?"

I laugh. "Pretty sure that's not in your job description. We'll figure it out."

"My offer still stands," Madison says with a wink. "Seriously, a date night would not be a bad idea."

I nod. "Yeah, you're probably right. Hey, speaking of, when are you moving in with Bryan?"

Madison rolls her eyes. "Not until after the wedding. I didn't want to give Ben the idea that it's okay to move in with anyone he dates, so we had it written into our divorce paperwork that neither of us could live with someone without being married."

I let out a low groan. "Dang. Who would have guessed you'd be the first one to run into that rule? Especially since he was the one with the affair and the love child."

"Not me, but it's fine. The girls are already picking out stuff for their new rooms. By the time April rolls around, we'll be ready to move right in."

"It's going to be here before we know it."

"I'm so ready," Madison says. "I think we all are."

* * *

Eric and I are sitting on the couch with Piper and Carson planted between us, both of them wearing the matching footed flannel pajamas I got them for Christmas. The movie we're watching, *Frosty the Snowman*, is nearing the end, which means our night will soon be ending as well.

In front of us are the remnants of the sheet pan nachos we shared for dinner, four mostly empty cups of hot cocoa, and two half-eaten Christmas cookies. Plus a small collection of torn wrapping paper from the small gifts we exchanged. I got the kids matching pajamas, and Eric got them each a small Lego set... Minecraft themed, of course.

He got me some new tools to use as I continue to dip my toes into the world of sourdough: a bench scraper and a scoring blade.

For him, I bought a shirt that says *This Dad Delivers.* When he opened it, he laughed, shaking his head before pulling me into a hug. "It's perfect," he said. "And so true."

Eric reaches over the back of the couch and squeezes my shoulder, causing me to look over at him. "I think we can call our first Christmas Eve together a success," he declares gently.

"I think so, too." I nod as the ending credits of the movie play. "But we have one more thing to do."

"What is it?" Carson asks with a yawn, crumbs from his half-cookie sticking to his face.

"We have to put out our reindeer food," I tell him. "I have

some for you and Piper to spread around in our yard, and then I also have some for you to take home and put in yours."

Carson looks confused. "What's reindeer food?"

"You don't know what reindeer food is?" Piper squeals in shock. "How do the reindeer even know to come to your house then?"

Carson shrugs. "I don't know. Daddy?"

Eric shakes his head, looking between me and Piper. "I don't know either, kiddo. Maybe we've just gotten lucky all these years. But we better go ahead and put some in our yard when we get home just in case."

I lead everyone into the kitchen and straight to the counter where I begin pulling out ingredients. I line three small Tupperware bowls on the counter. "First, we need oats. This is for the reindeer to eat." I scoop out half a cup of oatmeal into my bowl before refilling the measuring cup and handing it to Carson. He follows my lead, and then Piper does the same.

"Now, the glitter," I say, opening the glitter container and gently shaking it into my bowl.

"Glitter?" Carson exclaims. "You can't eat glitter!"

"Don't worry, they won't eat it," Piper assures him. "The reindeer see the glitter when it sparkles in the moonlight. That way, they know from way up high that we have food for them."

"Ohhh," Carson says with an understanding nod as I shake glitter into their bowls.

Next, I pick up the lids and place them on the bowls, ensuring they are screwed on tight. "Now we shake them up," I instruct, picking up my bowl and starting to shake.

The kids follow suit. "Now, I'm going to leave this here for Carson to take home. You guys bring your bowls, and we will go dump these in our yard."

Within minutes, the four of us are in the front yard. I help each kid open their lid, and they get to work diligently sprinkling the food in the grass.

"Mommy! It's so pretty. Our yard is all sparkly like a unicorn," Piper gushes.

"It really is," I agree. "You guys did great. Now, Santa will have no problem finding us."

"Dad, can we look and see where Santa is like we did last year?" Carson begs, hands folded together and looking up at Eric with a puppy dog face that could bring any man to his knees.

I turn to Eric with a raised brow, not following what Carson is asking for.

"The NORAD tracker shows where Santa is during his travels on Christmas night," he informs me. "It's something I've done with Carson since he was little."

"Well, what are we waiting for? Let's get my laptop," I announce.

We make our way inside, and while I pack up Carson's cookies and his reindeer food, Eric pulls up the radar.

"Where is he?" Piper asks, just above a whisper as though the big man himself is going to hear her.

"Well, it looks like he is just above Paris, France right now," Eric says, pointing at the screen.

"He's getting close!" Carson shouts excitedly. "We have to go home and get to bed so he doesn't miss us."

I turn to Piper. "He's right. You better work on getting tucked in, too."

Piper makes her way to Carson for a hug, as I turn to Eric. He pulls me in close and kisses my lips before gently pulling back.

I wrap my hands around his neck and rest my forehead on

his. "Tonight was so much fun," I tell him.

"It really was. I wouldn't mind celebrating many more just like this with you."

I nod, letting a soft smile land on my lips. "Me, too," I admit, before we are interrupted by the kids.

"Dad, we gotta go. Santa's going to skip our house if we don't hurry up," Carson groans, hopping from one foot to another with impatience.

"Okay, okay. We're going," Eric assures him, shaking his head before turning back to me. "Merry Christmas, Ava. I love you, and I'll talk to you tomorrow."

The smile on my face grows wider, and my heart speeds up just a little. He's never said those words to me before, and I admit I like hearing it. "Oh, you love me, huh?" I tease.

"I do. I really, really do," he assures me with a nod before planting a kiss on my forehead. "You're the best Christmas gift I could have ever asked for."

Without a pause, I lean in to kiss him one more time. "I love you, too."

As Eric and Carson head for the door and Piper skips toward the stairs, I take one last look at the glittering yard outside our window. This... the cookies, the cocoa, the kids' laughter, Eric's hand in mine... this is the kind of Christmas I've been longing for.

Chapter 19

"Mommy! Santa came!" Piper shouts excitedly, jumping up and down on my bed. "Come on. Get up! We have to go see what he left for us."

I let out a yawn and reach over to pick up my phone. "Piper, it's six-thirty in the morning. Can't you lay back down for another hour?" I plead.

"I know it's six-thirty. I set an alarm on my tablet to wake me up so we could open presents as early as possible."

I sit up and look at my seven-year-old, trying to hide the annoyance in my voice. "You set an alarm?"

"Yeah? So? You do it all the time."

"I set an alarm for us to get up for work and school," I argue.

"Well, this is better than school. More important, too. It's Christmas!"

I roll out of bed and follow Piper downstairs as she rushes straight to the stocking left for her by Santa.

I walk into the kitchen to start the coffee pot and then return to the room as she digs through her stocking. I take a seat on the couch while I wait for the coffee to brew. "What'd you get?"

"So much stuff," she says, excited, from behind the pile of stocking stuffers. "Lip gloss, a necklace, a pair of Minecraft socks, stickers, a book, and some candy!"

"It sounds like Santa knew exactly what you wanted this year," I tell her as she brings me the stocking I stuffed for myself the night before.

"Here. Open yours," she demands.

I make a show of pulling out my own gifts. "Let's see here. I got chocolate, lip gloss, lotion, hand sanitizer, a new can opener, and some nail polish. Santa did a good job here, too."

Piper pauses to look around the room. "Well, I don't see a sea otter tank," she mumbles.

"Well, maybe look around the tree. Maybe he hid it."

Piper makes her way to the side of the tree and bends down to pick something up, a stuffed sea otter toy. "Well, it's a sea otter, but not a real one. There's a note tied to his paw. Can you read it to me?"

I nod and hold out my hand to get the note and read it out loud to her.

Dear Piper,

I'm sorry, but I checked with the city and it is not legal to own a live sea otter within the city limits of Fawn Creek. However, check under the tree. I left you a bag with a small fish tank and some sea monkeys that you can grow all on your own. Hopefully that will be good enough until you're older and can convince the city to change their rules about marine life living in town.

Love, Santa

Piper makes her way to the tree, pulling out the sparkly red gift bag and peeking inside. She pauses to look at me before hugging her stuffed animal tight. "Well, I wish it was real, but a stuffy of Mr. Whiskers will have to do for now, I guess. And maybe I can grow my sea monkeys big enough that they can live in a tank in the garage."

I shake my head with a small laugh. "One can only hope."

Piper plops down beside me on the couch, clutching Mr. Whiskers to her chest. "This is the best Christmas ever," she announces.

I glance toward the kitchen where the coffee pot is just finishing and let out a quiet sigh, smiling to myself. "Yeah, kiddo. It really is."

* * *

"Thanks again for letting Piper come over this afternoon," Emilee says, holding the door open for Piper to step inside and race through the house to find Jacob. "Are you sure you don't want to stay for a little while?"

I shake my head. "I really appreciate the invite, but your niece woke me up at six-thirty this morning to open gifts. I think I'm going to head home and sneak in a nap before I pick her up this evening and take her to see my parents." I hand Emilee two gift bags. "These are for you and your parents, though."

Emilee takes the bags and peeks inside one. "Is this sourdough bread?" she asks, raising a brow as her mom joins us in the entryway.

I shrug. "Yes, just something new I've been playing around with. It's kind of fun."

Emilee hands Susanne a bag and continues to dig in her own. "What else is in here? Honey?"

"It's local honey. There's a small container of pink salt, too. Those two and a little bit of butter melted on the bread is incredible," I inform them. "Actually, I think I might go home and have a slice before my nap."

Susanne pulls me into a side hug. "Oh, sweet girl. I didn't know you were a baker."

I shrug. "I'm an amateur, really. It's just something I enjoy doing in my downtime."

"But still, it's amazing. I remember when I met you, you didn't even know how to heat up Ramen Noodles. You forgot to add water to the container and nearly burned down my kitchen," she teases.

I wrinkle my nose at the memory. "I'm still so embarrassed about that. But it was even more embarrassing when I had to go buy you a new microwave with money from my savings account because I caught yours on fire."

"I still can't believe your mom made you do that." She shakes her head with a chuckle. "I told her it wasn't necessary, but she didn't listen."

"She was adamant," I say with a laugh. "I get it now and would make Piper do the same, but back then I was so angry with her."

"Little did she know that we already loved you like you were one of ours," Susanne admits. "Then you gave us Piper, and I would have let you burn my whole house down in a heartbeat. I love you, Ava. No matter what happens in life, you will always be one of my kids."

"I love you, too," I say, pulling her into a hug. "I'm so lucky to have a bonus mom in you."

* * *

"Hey, sis," my brother Caleb says as I make my way into my parents' house, dragging along an armful of gift bags. "You know you're allowed to make more than one trip from the car, right?" he asks, helping by taking half of my bags.

"I know," I groan. "But it's okay. I got it all. That's what matters."

"Yeah, well, you probably dislocated your shoulder while you were at it," he grumbles, leading me into the living room.

"Yeah, yeah. If you're weak, just say that," I say with a laugh, taking a seat next to Tosha on the couch. Piper, who had raced into the house ahead of me, is sitting on the floor engrossed in a Lego set with my nephews, Asher and Maddox.

"What are you guys building?" I ask the kids.

"A rocket ship," Maddox informs me. "And I want Asher to make a space station, but he's too busy building a dumb old tower instead."

"I'm making a princess castle," Piper informs me.

"Well, princess castles can't be blue and red," Maddox says.

"They can be any color the princess wants. And this princess likes blue and red, thank you very much," Piper snaps back.

Tosha and I exchange a look. "Oh good, two hard-headed children. What fun," I mutter.

"They both definitely get that from you," Caleb says, not looking up from his phone.

I pick up a nearby throw pillow and toss it in his direction. "Ha! Me? I'm not the stubborn one."

"Yeah right, Ava. You just carried in seventy-five pounds worth of Christmas gifts into the house at once because you were too stubborn to make an extra trip back to the car," he argues.

I roll my eyes. "I think they get some of that from the rest of the Montgomery side of the family, not just me."

All eyes in the room dart toward my mom, who is sitting on

the couch watching the kids play. "What? I wasn't listening," she admits.

"We were just wondering where the kids... and Ava get their stubbornness from," Caleb tells her.

"Well, not me." She waves us off. "Must be your father."

I raise a brow. "Oh really? Because I seem to remember you trying to move a mattress because Dad didn't do it fast enough, and then you got it stuck in the staircase. You couldn't get out and had to stand there for two hours, trapped, while you waited for me and Caleb to get home to help you."

"Thank God we didn't have to rely on you to pick us up from school. We would have been there for hours," Caleb says with a laugh. "The school probably would have called CPS on you."

Mom groans. "Well, I did get my first cell phone after that and never got stuck in a staircase again. Plus, the bed got moved, didn't it?"

Caleb shakes his head. "Yep, she definitely didn't get that stubbornness from you, Mom."

"Anyway, now that everyone is here," Tosha says, sitting up straighter on the couch, "Caleb and I have an announcement."

I exchange a look with my sister-in-law, half hoping she's going to send me a subliminal message instead of making me wait thirty seconds to find out the news with everyone else.

"After we came home to visit on Thanksgiving, we started to do some looking around, and I decided to apply for a job closer to home," Caleb explains. "I had my final interview yesterday, and they offered me the job. After the new year, I will officially be working in Owen for an oil company in the marketing department."

Mom's jaw drops open as she processes the information. "You're moving home?!" she squeals, jumping up from the couch faster than I ever would have guessed possible for a woman her age. "This is so exciting!"

"Congratulations," I say to my brother and sister-in-law, standing up to hug Tosha.

"I was hoping maybe a certain real estate agent could help us find a place here in Fawn Creek?" Tosha asks with a wink.

"I'd love to. I already have a list in my head," I tell her.

Piper looks up from her Lego castle, grinning. "See? I told you this would be the best Christmas ever."

I glance around the room at my parents, my brother and sister-in-law, and Piper giggling with her cousins and I can't help but agree.

"Yeah," I say softly, more to myself than anyone else. "It really is."

Chapter 20

It's the morning after Christmas, and I'm running on caffeine and a prayer, trying to get back into the swing of things. School is out and daycare is closed, so I'm camped at the dining room table with my laptop open. Piper is sitting beside me with her new art set. While I juggle calls and schedule a few showings for Caleb and Tosha, my phone buzzes. The group text is already firing up for the day.

Sierra: Hey, what's everyone doing for New Year's Eve? Short Creek has live music that night.

Tyler: Count us in, hopefully. I'll see if my mom can keep Molly. Andrew and I are way overdue for a date night.

Ava: I can't. No sitter. Caleb and Tosha have already claimed my parents this year, and they'll be in Colorado for New Year's.

Madison: I'll keep Piper. And Carson. I'll keep Juliet and Molly too!

Ava: Madison, that doesn't seem fair. You'd have all of our kids while we go out without you.

Madison: Does it make you feel better to know I'm going to charge you? I need to make some extra money for wedding stuff and our trip next month. I was going to offer another

parents' night out event anyway, so you'd basically be doing me a favor. They can all stay the night, and you can pick them up in the morning.

Avery: Madi, are you sure? That's a lot of kids overnight.

Madison: I spend every day with them. I'd rather have our crew than a bunch of kids I don't know.

Tyler: Okay, let's do it. And Avery can be our designated driver.

Avery: Sure! Might as well take full advantage of my situation.

Sierra: I'll buy you all the shots of Dr. Pepper you could ever want.

I set my phone down with a grin I can't hide. A kid-free night with Eric, live music, and my favorite people? It sounds like the perfect way to ring in the new year.

* * *

"Okay, was there anything else in town you were wanting to see?" I ask Caleb and Tosha as we finish the walkthrough on the final house. This one is conveniently right down the street from mine.

"No, I think we're good." Caleb glances at Tosha, who nods.

"Absolutely. I think we're going to grab lunch and talk things over. Wanna join us? I've been dying for some Rio Escondido. I still dream about their flan," Tosha says with a grin.

"I'd love to, but I have a few things to finish before I pick up Piper from Mom."

"That's okay. We'll text you and let you know which house

151

we want to make an offer on."

"Perfect. Then we can meet at my office to get the offer ready."

I'm just pulling into my driveway when a familiar delivery truck stops at the curb.

"Well, fancy meeting you here." Eric climbs out with a package and grins. "Having a good day?"

I meet him in the yard and give him a quick kiss. "Yes, and somehow it's even better now."

"Me too." He smiles. "I was ready with a dad joke, and now I have to save it for next time. Knowing you, I'll be back in a few days."

"Oh no, I need it now," I say, crossing my arms.

"It doesn't work unless I say it to the doorbell."

I hand the package back. "Be my guest."

Eric steps onto the porch, presses the doorbell, and leans toward the camera. "Hey Ava. Why did the snowman ring the doorbell? Because he heard the hottest girl in town was inside and he wanted to cool her off."

I groan as he turns back, looking entirely too proud of himself.

"What? That was good."

I shake my head. "That was... something."

"How dare you pretend that isn't funny."

I kiss his cheek. "I wasn't pretending."

"I can't believe I fell in love with a woman with no sense of humor."

"And I can't believe I love a man who tells such awful jokes."

Eric laughs and hands me the package. "I have to get back to work. I saw your text about New Year's Eve and I'm in."

"Good. Madison's planning noisemakers, special food,

movies, and dance parties. She might have more fun than the kids. And if you wanted to, you could stay that night. Then we'll pick up the kids in the morning and grab breakfast together."

"There's nothing I want more than to start the new year by waking up next to you. Count me in."

I watch Eric drive away and then bolt for my front door, fumbling with the keypad. I can't get inside fast enough.

I yank out my phone, scroll to Sierra's name, and hit call. She answers on the second ring.

"Hey. What's up?" she asks, the background noise of *The Office* muffled behind her.

"You busy?"

"No, unless eating my weight in Christmas cookies counts as busy. What's wrong?"

"So, Eric is coming to Short Creek on New Year's Eve."

"As he should..."

"And he's staying the night." I pace the living room, my voice a little too high-pitched.

"Okay? None of this sounds like an emergency."

"Sierra, this absolutely is an emergency."

"I'm gonna need you to explain this to me like I'm five."

I flop onto the couch with a dramatic groan. "I can't tell a five-year-old what Eric and I will be doing that night. For the first time ever."

"Wait." Sierra's voice jumps an octave. "You two haven't done it yet?"

I shake my head, even though she can't see me. "Nope."

"But... how?"

"Because we always have kids with us. You can't just leave a four- and seven-year-old unsupervised so you can run off to get it on."

Sierra laughs. "Nobody says 'get it on' anymore."

"I'm a little out of practice, okay?"

She pauses. "Wait. You haven't been celibate this whole time since Zach's accident, have you?"

"Of course not," I groan. "There have been... moments. But Eric is different. I really like him. I want our first time to be perfect. I feel like I need to shave my entire body, get a spray tan, maybe cut my hair. Do I need bangs? Should I wax my eyebrows? Oh my gosh, should I join a gym?"

Sierra snorts. "The gym? What are you training for, the Olympics? You do have it bad for this guy. But no, you don't need a spray tan. You're the perfect shade of bronze already. We literally just trimmed your hair two weeks ago and if you cut those curtain bangs, I will disown you. Your eyebrows are perfect. I'll send you the link to my esthetician. Get a good wax and you'll feel brand new."

I sigh. "Okay."

"Seriously, you're perfect. Eric's not thinking about your eyebrows. He's thinking about you. Now go book your appointment and chill."

"I know. It's just been a while..."

"It's just like riding a bike. You'll remember how it all works once you..."

"Hold on," I interrupt, laughing. "Caleb just texted. He and Tosha are ready to make an offer on their house. I've gotta go meet them."

"Then go sell a house and order some sexy panties off Amazon. This is not a granny-panty occasion."

"Got it. Appointment, panties, house. Easy."

* * *

"Okay, you guys. Have fun with Miss Madi tonight and be good," I tell Piper and Carson as Eric and I drop them off at Madison's. "We'll come back to pick you up in the morning."

"They'll be fine," Madison assures me. "We have a full night planned. I won't be surprised if they don't even make it til midnight, but we'll see."

Eric and I say our goodbyes and head back to my house for dinner before a night out with our friends.

"It smells amazing in here," Eric says, following me into the kitchen.

"Thanks! I tried my hand at sourdough garlic bread to go with chicken alfredo and a side salad," I say, pulling the casserole dish from the oven. "I'm really having too much fun playing around with this whole sourdough thing."

"And I'm having a lot of fun being your guinea pig," he laughs. "If I didn't know better, I'd say you're trying to fatten me up."

I wink as I make plates for us. "I'll never tell."

* * *

"Hey!" Sierra calls out across the crowded bar, waving.

Avery, Derek, Eric, and I carpooled to Short Creek tonight, meeting Tyler, Andrew, Cody, and Sierra as soon as we arrive.

"You look amazing," Sierra says, pulling me close as I make my way over. "How are you feeling? Still nervous?"

I shake my head, glancing around the bar. "No, I'm okay. The initial freak-out has worn off. I'm doing a lot better now. What are you drinking?" I ask, eyeing the bright blue drink in her cup.

Sierra holds it up so I can get a closer look. "It's an ocean water. Coconut rum, Curaçao, and Sprite," she explains, handing it to me. "Try it. Blue is my favorite flavor."

I take a small sip. "Okay, yeah, that's good."

"Right? It's like the slushies I was obsessed with in high school, but the grown-up version."

"Hey, babe," Eric interrupts, kissing the side of my head. "I'm going to get a beer. Want anything?"

"One of those," I say, pointing to Sierra's cup.

"Just tell them an ocean water," Sierra says as "Copperhead Road" starts playing across the bar. "We're needed on the dance floor." She sets her drink down in front of Cody and pulls me onto the sawdust floor. "Hope you're ready for a night of dancing, my friend."

I laugh. "Just don't wear me out too much. I have important things to do tonight."

* * *

"Okay, ladies and gentlemen. Three minutes until midnight. It's time to ring in the new year!" the DJ's voice booms. "Grab a complimentary glass of champagne and get ready for the countdown."

Sierra, Tyler, Avery, and I step off the dance floor and head to the boys, seated on bar stools along the edge, keeping an eye on our drinks.

I toss my long, dark hair into a ponytail and lean in to kiss Eric, only to be interrupted as a waitress arrives with a tray of plastic champagne flutes. We each take one and set it on the counter, waiting for the countdown to begin.

"Tonight was perfect," I tell him softly. "Thanks for coming with me."

Eric smiles down at me, his eyes lighting up. "Always. I wouldn't be anywhere else."

The crowd begins counting together. "5... 4... 3... 2... 1..."

I feel his arms wrap around me just as the group shouts, "Happy New Year!" The room erupts in cheers, but for a moment, it's just him and me. I tip my glass to him, and he tips his back with me.

"I love you," I whisper, resting my forehead against his.

"Love you, too. Happy New Year, baby. And many more," he replies, pressing a kiss to my lips. The kind of kiss that has me aching for more.

The noise of the bar returns, friends laughing and cheering all around us, but I can't stop smiling. This might just be the best year of my life.

* * *

"Avery, thanks again for offering to drive all of us home," I say, climbing into the third row of her SUV.

She waves me off. "No problem at all. I had fun watching all of you act like fools tonight."

"Seriously, though. Thank you. We needed a night out more than I realized," Tyler chimes in. "And Madi keeping the kids overnight is just icing on the cake. I cannot wait to start the new year by sleeping in past six in the morning."

Avery looks back at us in the rearview mirror. "I still feel kind of bad for leaving Juliet with Madi all night. I mean, I didn't drink tonight. I could easily pick her up and take her home."

"Nope," Derek answers immediately. "You will leave her there and give yourself a chance to sleep in tomorrow. Besides, Madi already said that if you show up to get her and wake up the other kids she is going to egg our house."

Avery shakes her head and puts the car in drive to pull out of the parking lot. "She wouldn't."

"She might," I inform Avery. "Can you imagine trying to get all of those kids to fall asleep? Then only to have someone show up and wake them? Nope, don't chance it."

Avery pulls into the long driveway where Tyler and Sierra's houses are, putting the car in park for them and their husbands to climb out.

"Thanks for the ride, Avery." Sierra waves to her before leaning across the car to look at me. "Have fun tonight," she winks.

Thank God for the overhead light in the car turning off just in time for my face to turn what I can only imagine to be a deep shade of crimson.

"Have fun doing what?" Derek asks from the front seat with a very clear tone of confusion.

Eric nearly chokes trying to fight back laughter as Avery lets out a groan.

"What?" Derek asks, still confused.

"Shush," Avery whispers loudly. "I'll explain later."

Thankfully, Derek takes the hint and turns on the radio to fill the awkward silence in the car with the sound of '90s country music instead. I mean, nothing can put a girl in the mood quite like Shania Twain's *Man, I Feel Like a Woman.*

Just a few minutes later, we are parked in my driveway where Eric and I climb out of the back of the SUV.

"Thanks again, Avery, for the ride," Eric says, holding out his hand to help me climb down from the car. "Enjoy your sleep."

"She will," Derek responds. "Night, guys."

Eric and I make our way into the house, pausing to kick our

shoes off at the front door. Suddenly, I feel like I've never been alone in a house with a man before.

What do I do? Offer him a beer? Do I even have beer? Maybe offer him a snack? No, he's not a six-year-old.

Eric raises a brow and looks at me. "You okay?"

I nod, trying to calm my racing heart. "Yeah, I'm just realizing that I've never actually been alone with you before. Not like this."

He squeezes my hand. "Well, that's not a bad thing."

I shake my head. "No, definitely not. Just a new thing."

He smirks. "I like new things with you."

"Me too," I confess. "Are you hungry? Thirsty? Tired?"

He smiles softly, still holding on to my hand as he pulls me in closer to him. He rests his forehead against mine and pauses. "Ava, you don't have to entertain me. I'm not a guest at a party. Relax."

I can feel the warmth of his breath on my face and my heart does that ridiculous fluttery thing again. "I... I don't know what I'm supposed to do right now," I admit softly.

Eric chuckles. "Nothing. You don't have to do anything. Just... this. Be here with me. You're all I need." He brushes a loose strand of hair behind my ear and softly kisses my lips.

Just as he pulls away, I lean forward for more. I've been so worried about getting to this moment with him tonight that I almost forgot to enjoy the time leading up to it.

"I love you," I whisper, "and I'm so glad you're here."

"Me too, baby. There's nowhere else in the world I'd rather be."

* * *

"Good morning," Eric whispers into my ear, wrapping his arms around me and pulling me close. "How'd you sleep?"

Slowly, I open my eyes, taking a moment to realize where I am and who is lying beside me. I lean back and kiss his cheek, letting his beard softly tickle my skin. "So good. Better than I have in a long time," I admit, unsure whether it's the lingering buzz from last night or sleeping next to someone other than Piper for the first time in over seven years.

"Last night was fun," Eric murmurs, pressing a gentle kiss to my neck and holding me close.

"I have a feeling you aren't just talking about the bar."

He chuckles softly. "I wasn't. The bar was fun, sure, but coming home with you? That was even better. I wouldn't mind doing that more often."

"Neither would I," I admit, snuggling closer. "What time is it?"

"Ten 'til nine."

I pause. "I can't remember the last time I slept this late."

"Well, we had a busy night," he teases.

"Indeed we did," I sigh with visions of the two of us tangled in the sheets flashing through my mind. I shake my head. "I need a shower, and we need to get the kids."

He kisses my cheek and sits up. "I'll get dressed and handle the kids. You shower, and then we'll make breakfast. Sound good?"

"I can go..." I start, pushing into a seated position, but Eric stops me.

"No. Ava, go shower. Take your time. Relax. Let me take care of things. You focus on you, and I'll help with the rest."

I bite my lip. "I'm not used to letting anyone help me."

Eric bends down to kiss my forehead. "I know. And we're

going to change that. I'm here now, and I'm helping, like it or not."

Chapter 21

"Okay, Mom. I'm about to run into the store. Do you need anything?" I say into my phone as I pull into the parking lot at the Fawn Creek Market.

She laughs. "Nope. We are set on eggs, bread, and milk over here. You don't really think we are going to get that much snow, do you?"

"I don't know. I really wouldn't mind a snow day," I admit.

"I'm pretty sure your job doesn't stop for snow."

"It doesn't. But that's one of the beautiful things about being my own boss," I tell her. "I knew this winter storm was approaching, so I tied up all my loose strings and brought my laptop home just in case. If we get the eight inches of snow that Travis Meyer is predicting, I'll be ready. Well, just as soon as I stop at the store."

"Okay, well, don't let me keep you then. For what it's worth, I hope you get your snow day tomorrow. You always loved them when you were young."

I scoff. "Mom, I'm still young and don't you forget it." I remind her before saying goodbye and slipping my phone into my purse. I step out into the grocery store parking lot and the cold air burns against my face. It definitely feels like we are in for some winter weather.

Once inside the grocery store, I grab a cart and point it toward the dairy section when a voice behind the checkout counter calls out to me.

"Hope you don't need bread. We're sold out," Stephanie, the grocery store manager, informs me.

I shake my head as I turn to face her. "No, thankfully I'm in my sourdough era right now, and I have a few loaves in the freezer already."

Stephanie looks shocked. "Oh."

"What?"

"Oh, nothing." She shakes her head. "I just never pictured you as a bake-bread-from-scratch kind of person. Didn't you set off the smoke alarm in the home ec room in tenth grade?"

I sigh. "Yeah, that was me."

Stephanie scowls. "I had to stand outside in the sleet in my cheer uniform for half an hour."

"Yeah, sorry about that. If it makes you feel better, I have not set off a commercial smoke alarm in a very long time," I inform her proudly.

"Hey, I bet that hunky UPS man is enjoying all of your baking," Stephanie says, wiggling her eyebrows. "I hear things are pretty serious with you guys."

I rock back and forth on my heels, looking over my shoulder toward the dairy aisle. I truly thought I'd be in and out of here in just a few minutes. I should have known better. "Um, yeah. You could say that."

"So, when's the big day?"

I furrow my brows, confused by the question. "What big day? Madison's?"

Stephanie laughs, busying herself with straightening items on the shelf next to her. "No, yours, silly."

"I don't know what you're talking about."

"You and Eric. When are you going to get married?"

"We aren't really planning anything like that anytime soon," I tell her. "We just started dating in October." I don't mention to her that we only had sex for the first time two weeks ago.

Now it's her turn to furrow her brow. "Are you sure?"

"As far as I know."

She shakes her head. "No, I heard that you guys were engaged, and as soon as you get married you are going to become a stay-at-home mom. I didn't believe it at first, but it makes sense with the homemade bread thing. Like you're training."

I let out a groan. "Steph, you heard wrong. Eric and I are not engaged. We are dating and happy, but have no plans to get married anytime soon."

She frowns at this information, and I continue.

"Also, I'm one of the top real estate agents in Montgomery County. I have my own brokerage. I love my job and have no plans to quit, no matter what happens in the future with my love life."

Stephanie nods. "I'm sorry. You know how gossip is around here. That's just what someone said, and I should have known better than to listen."

I wave her off. "It's fine. I'm not upset, and yes, I know how talk is around here." I assure her. "I promise you, I did not work this hard to build my business to throw it all away the second I met someone. I truly love what I do, and I can see myself doing it for the rest of my life. But right now, I really need to get some milk and eggs and ingredients for chicken noodles so I can get back home."

"Okay, I'll get out of your way and let you shop. If I don't see you again, be careful out there. I heard the roads could get pretty bad."

"You be careful too!" I call back, pushing my cart around the corner. "Stay warm!"

* * *

"So, she just point blank asked if you are going to quit your job and become a housewife?" Madison clarifies. "Does she not know who you are?"

"I would think she does. We've only known each other since preschool. I am just flabbergasted that this is what the people of Fawn Creek are choosing to gossip about. Is this what people really think of me? That I would give up that easy?"

Madison shakes her head as she wipes down her kitchen counter and presses the start button on the dishwasher. It hums to life before she turns to cross her arms in front of her chest and face me. "Well, you have to admit, you've stayed back in the shadows since Zach passed away. Now that you are falling in love with a new guy, I think the town is mostly just rooting for you. Everyone wants to see you have a happily ever after."

"Me, too. Believe me, and I really do think I'll get it this time. I just need everyone to chill while I get there."

Madison smiles. "Sorry, friend. We have no chill when it comes to seeing you thriving."

"I've noticed." I smirk, looking around the kitchen. "What do you think? Are we going to have school tomorrow? Is the storm going to be as bad as they say?"

Madison shrugs. "I'm betting on a snow day, which means

nothing to me. As long as kids can get here, I'll be open."

I frown. "Well, that's no fun."

"It's fine. I won't have a full house, and I usually end up having a fun day with the kids that do make it. Besides, I still need to make money."

"Well, if there's no school, count on Piper staying home. I'm going to let her sleep in all day if I can. I'll pay you for the day, of course, but I'm going to enjoy a true snow day with her." I smirk. "I have hot cocoa, ingredients for chicken noodles, and bread to bake."

"It sounds like a perfect, cozy day." Madison smiles. "Now, just you wait. We won't get a single snowflake."

"We'll see."

* * *

The sound of my phone vibrating on my nightstand wakes me from a deep sleep. It's five in the morning, and Eric is texting me.

Eric: Hey, sorry if this wakes you up. Just trying to figure out what I'm going to do today. Do you think Madison will be open? There's like nine inches of snow on the ground and I have to leave town early. I was wondering if you could keep Carson for me until she opens.

I read over the text once and then once again. *Nine inches? Seriously?*

I climb out of bed and move the curtain to peek out the window, confirming what Eric is telling me. Everything as far as I can see is a solid sheet of snow. The trees, the streets, the rooftops. It's early enough that there aren't even tire tracks along the road in front of my house. There for sure will not be school today. I pick the phone back up and fire off a text to Eric.

Ava: Hey. It's fine. Madison will be open regardless of the weather, and yes, I could keep him this morning. But why don't you just let me keep Carson all day? What do we think about giving her a paid day off and you can drop Carson off here? Madison hasn't had a true snow day with her girls as long as she's done daycare.

Eric: Absolutely. But, are you sure you don't mind keeping him? My parents could do it, they are home, but Carson gets so bored with them all day. And I need to head out sooner rather than later.

Ava: I'm sure. Bring him on over whenever, and he can stay as long as he needs to. Piper will be glad to have someone to play with.

Within half an hour, I'm sitting on the couch with a cup of coffee in my comfiest lounge set when I hear Eric's tires crunch into the snow in front of my house. I open the door and watch as Eric lifts Carson out of the car and carries him toward my porch. Carson is still wearing his footie Spiderman pajamas.

"Hey," I smile as they make their way toward me and I hold open the screen door.

Eric gives me a quick kiss and then hands over the sleeping child. Carson immediately nuzzles into my neck, not even waking up as he's transferred to me.

"Thank you for doing this, seriously," he says, shrugging off the oversized duffle bag hanging off his arm. "Everything is in here. Coat, boots, gloves, hat. Extra clothes, his blankie. You know, all the things. I tried to make this as easy as possible for you."

I wave him off. "We're going to have a great day. You just be careful and don't worry about us." I assure him. "I love you."

"I love you," he replies, kissing me one more time before pausing to kiss the side of Carson's head. Carson just snores lightly into my shoulder, still unbothered by what's happening around him.

"He might be a little freaked out when he wakes up not at home. Just a warning."

I nod. "I'll make sure I'm close by. Now, go. I'll see you tonight and I'll have dinner ready."

Eric frowns. "It might be late."

"I have nowhere else to be."

* * *

It's just after nine in the morning and my kitchen is filled with the scent of vanilla and cinnamon while I work on preparing a stack of French toast for the kids. Just as I'm sliding the last slice onto a plate, the sound of a crying child rings through the house.

"Mom! Carson's awake!" Piper shouts out to me from the living room.

"Thanks, Piper. I had no idea," I mutter under my breath as I make my way into the room.

"Hey buddy. It's okay," I say, taking a seat next to him on the sofa.

Carson looks at me with a quivering lip before he grabs his

blanket and crawls into my lap. "Where's my daddy?" he asks with a sniffle.

I gently smooth his hair as he gets comfortable against me, his crying subsiding thankfully. "Dad's at work. It snowed today, a whole lot, and you guys don't have school, so you're spending the day with me and Piper."

"Okay," he whispers, taking the news much easier than I expected him to.

He trusts me. And honestly, that means as much to me as I'm sure it does to him.

"It was probably pretty scary to wake up and not know where you were. You were very sleepy when your dad brought you over to my house this morning," I tell him.

"I was?"

"You were. And it was still dark outside," I confirm. "But we are going to have a fun day together. Do you want to look outside and see the snow?"

Carson nods and scrambles out of my lap, running toward the window next to the door. "Whoa. That's a lot of snow."

"Yeah, it is."

"Can me and Piper build a snowman?" he asks excitedly, his tears from moments ago already forgotten.

I nod. "Yes. Later today, when it warms up a little, we will go outside and play. But right now, who is ready for some French toast?"

"Me!" both kids respond in unison.

"Well, off to the table then," I say, pointing the way. "We have a full day of fun planned, and we can't do it without full bellies."

* * *

"Okay, Carson, come here and I'll help you reach the snowman to put his nose in place." I scoop him up, waiting as he presses the carrot into the middle of the snowman's head.

"My turn!" Piper calls, her mittened hands full of rocks she collected from the yard.

I set Carson back on the ground and lift Piper next, holding her steady while she presses in the rocks to give our snowman a wide smile and lopsided eyes.

When we step back to admire our work, Piper sighs happily. "Beautiful."

"Awesome," Carson adds, before turning to me. "I'm hungry again."

I grin. "Your little nose is pink, so I think it's time to go in and get warmed up anyway."

I snap a quick photo of the kids with their snowman, then usher them toward the house. The porch is slick with slush, and our boots squeak against the mat as we kick them off. The moment we step inside, we're greeted by the sweet, buttery smell of the chocolate chip cookies we left cooling before heading out.

"The cookies smell sooooo good!" Piper groans, tugging off her hat, coat, and gloves.

"The smell is making my tummy grumbly," Carson adds.

"Mine too," I say, laughing. "But first, let's get you two into warm, dry clothes. Piper, go put on some cozy jammies and bring your jeans down so I can throw them in the dryer."

"Okay!" she shouts, thundering up the stairs.

I sit on the couch in front of Carson and help him wriggle out of his snow-covered pants and back into his jammies.

"Thanks for helping us build Mr. Snowman," he says with a sleepy smile.

"You're welcome. You guys did a great job." I ruffle his damp hair. "Now, hop under this blanket and get warm while I make cocoa and grab you a cookie."

Carson obeys, climbing under the blanket with a satisfied little sigh. I scoop up his wet clothes and toss them in the dryer just as Piper comes skipping back down with hers.

Soon the hum of the dryer fills the background while I whisk cocoa on the stove and stack two cookies on each napkin. My fingers are still stinging from the cold when I carry the tray into the living room.

"Carson, you're so funny!" Piper giggles as I set the snacks down. Both kids are bundled in blankets, jammies on, controllers in hand, already lost in the world of Minecraft.

"This is the best snow day ever," Carson says with a grin, cheeks still pink from the cold.

I pause for a moment, just watching them. There's a warmth in my chest that has nothing to do with the cocoa I've been sipping on.

* * *

"Hey," I whisper, keeping my voice low to avoid waking the kids while Eric steps inside. The cold winter air follows him in, causing me to tighten my cardigan around my body to avoid the chill.

Eric leans forward, kissing my lips, his cold nose grazing mine. "I'm so sorry it's so late. The roads are worse now than they were this morning. Everything thawed today and then froze right back over. I don't think they are going to school tomorrow either."

I close the door and usher him into the house. "It's fine. I'm glad you made it back. You probably should have just gotten a hotel closer to work."

Eric frowns. "Probably. But Carson was here, and I didn't want you stuck with him all night after having him all day."

I pull Eric into the living room and motion toward Carson, who is snoozing quietly on the sofa.

"He would have been okay," I inform him with a smirk.

"You must have worn him out today." Eric shakes his head. "He doesn't go to sleep easily, ever. And he probably won't go back to sleep after I get him home."

"Then don't take him home." I shrug.

Eric frowns. "I can't just leave him here."

"You can stay, too," I suggest. "I mean, if you want to. No pressure. You can even sleep in the guest room if you don't want to answer questions from two curious kids in the morning."

"And miss the chance to sleep next to you? Not happening." Eric grins.

"Okay, Romeo. But first, how about dinner? I saved you some homemade chicken and noodles. Plus, the kids baked some delicious cookies today."

Eric's shoulders relax noticeably. "Oh my gosh. You are officially my favorite person on the planet. All I've had today is a bag of chips, beef jerky, and a Red Bull."

I shake my head. "And I'll be sending you with leftovers for lunch tomorrow. Come on. Let's get you fed."

Within ten minutes, Eric is seated at the table, finishing his plate of chicken noodles, mashed potatoes, and a homemade roll. "That was the best thing I've eaten in a long time," he says as he places his fork down on his empty plate.

"I'd love to take that as a compliment, but you literally just ate chips and jerky for your last meal sooo..." I tease.

Eric chuckles, shaking his head. "Still. You're spoiling me."

"Get used to it," I say softly as I collect his plate and make my way toward the kitchen.

He stands and moves behind me, sliding his arms around my waist as I rinse the dish. "You know, I think I could get used to this," he murmurs, his chin brushing against my shoulder.

I turn in his arms, smiling up at him. "Good. Because I like taking care of you."

"Careful," he teases. "Say stuff like that and I might never leave."

"That's not exactly a threat."

His grin is soft as he kisses me once more. "Come on. Let's go to bed. I want to sleep next to you before it's morning and we're back to reality."

"Okay," I whisper, following him toward the stairs. I could definitely get used to this.

Chapter 22

One month later.

"Madi... this place is spectacular." I step through the doorway into our beach house on Tybee Island, pausing just to take it all in. The main living area is airy and bright, with wide-plank floors and walls painted a soft, beachy blue. French doors at the back open to a deck, and beyond that, the ocean glints in the distance.

"Seriously, the pictures did not do it justice," Tyler says, brushing past me and spinning slowly in the center of the room. "I might not ever be able to go back home. We just got here and I'm already in love with this place."

"At six hundred dollars a night, I think you'll be just fine to stay for the weekend and then go back home." Andrew drops his duffel on the floor with a smirk.

Tyler shoots him a look but doesn't argue, just flips her hair over her shoulder. "Anyway, what's the plan for tonight?"

Madison sets her tote bag on the counter and pulls out her phone, already scrolling. "I thought we could freshen up, head downtown for an early dinner at Pier 91, then maybe grab alcoholic slushies from Wet Willies and walk the beach."

Derek leans against the doorframe, one brow raised. "Wait, you can walk around with an open container here?"

"Hell yes, you can," Bryan says with a grin, dropping onto the couch like he owns the place. "It's one of the best things about Tybee and Savannah, too. No glass on the beach, of course, but a cold can of beer by the water? Heaven."

Madison nods, her expression softening as she looks around the space. "This whole place is laid back. That's how Bryan sold me on it. They don't call it 'Running on Tybee Time' for nothing. And listen, you guys are free to do whatever you want. Don't feel like you have to stick together the whole time. We can each do our own thing and just meet back for meals. We could even do a little cooking here to save some money."

I wander into the kitchen, running my fingers over the smooth white granite countertops. "Good plan. And I don't mind helping with food prep either. I'd love to spend a couple of days pretending this is my kitchen."

"Well, I vote we all stick together tonight," Avery says, stretching her legs out in front of her. "Tomorrow we can split up if we want. Between two rental cars and the fact that the island's only three miles wide, we should be good."

Madison claps her hands together. "Perfect. I'll grab groceries tomorrow so we have stuff here."

"I'll go with you," I say quickly. "I don't get to cook much at home, and I want to take advantage of it while we're here. Besides, you already do so much cooking for the kids. This is your vacation. Let us take care of you."

Madison's face softens, and for a moment it feels like the trip has really started.

* * *

"Now this is something I could get used to," Tyler says as we walk along the beach, her flip-flops dangling from her fingers. The damp sand is cool beneath my feet, and the sound of waves crashing against the shore feels almost unreal after so many months of gray Kansas skies.

"I can't believe I'm barefoot on the beach in January," Tyler adds. "Earlier this week I was sleeping with a heated blanket. Andrew, I'm serious. Let's move here."

Andrew snorts, shoving his hands in his pockets. "Ty, I already pulled up the Realtor app when we were eating dinner. If we sold everything we owned, we could maybe afford to rent a beach house for one summer."

Tyler groans dramatically, tossing her head back toward the stars. "Fine. My beach house dreams can wait a little longer. Until I win the lottery." She glances at me with a grin. "Remind me to start playing the lottery."

I chuckle, tucking my hands into the sleeves of my cardigan. "Will do."

Avery bends to pick up a smooth white shell and holds it up to examine it. "So, what's everyone wanting to do tomorrow?"

Bryan is the first to answer. "I went ahead and booked a fishing charter for all the guys. We'll be gone from sunrise until after lunch, so you ladies will have the house all to yourselves."

"Don't forget we're doing a ghost tour tomorrow night," Madison adds, her eyes glinting in the moonlight. "Tickets are for eight-thirty. I figured we'd grab dinner in downtown Savannah before heading to the tour."

Cody slows his steps, grimacing. "Am I the only one who finds this whole ghost tour thing a little weird?"

"Oh, baby. Are you scared?" Sierra teases, bumping him playfully with her hip. "I'll protect you."

Madison shakes her head, laughing. "If we're doing Savannah, we have to do a ghost tour. It's the whole reason Bryan suggested this trip in the first place. If we hadn't had the kids with us when we were in Galveston, we would've done one there too."

Avery lifts a brow. "Madi, I had no idea you were into spooky stuff. I thought you only liked romcoms and chick flicks."

Madison grins. "You're mostly right, but there's more to me than what's on the pink glittery surface."

"Oh goodness," Tyler chimes in. "You'd be shocked at some of the stuff she buys in my bookstore. She acts all wholesome and then bam... she throws a thriller into her book stack like it's nothing."

"It's called balance!" Madison protests. "You can enjoy both love and murder."

Bryan shoots her a wide-eyed look. "Wow. There's a lot I need to learn about you before the wedding. If I ever go missing, you guys better remember she's been studying how to hide a body."

Laughter ripples through the group. I hook my arm through Madison's and smirk at Bryan. "Forget it, buddy. If she deems you unworthy, we have no choice but to trust her gut and help her hide the body. That's what friends are for."

Sierra raises her plastic cup, the icy contents sloshing. "To love, laughter, and plausible deniability."

* * *

"Okay, I'm going to take a shower and get to bed. Sunrise will be here before we know it," Bryan says, pushing himself out of the Adirondack chair on the back porch.

177

"I'm coming, too," Madison adds, stretching as she stands. "Today wore me out."

"Night, friends," I call softly as they disappear into the house, leaving Eric and me alone on the outdoor loveseat.

I grab the blanket draped over the back, spreading it across both of our laps before snuggling under the crook of his arm. The air smells like salt and sea grass, and the steady rhythm of the waves feels like it's syncing with my heartbeat.

"This is perfect," I murmur.

"No place I'd rather be," Eric says, kissing the top of my head. "How did I get so lucky?"

"Pretty sure I'm the lucky one." I snake my fingers through his and lean into him, letting the warmth of his side soak through me.

For a while, neither of us speaks. The only sounds are the ocean and the faint hum of voices drifting through the house. My heart feels full, like this is exactly where I'm meant to be and who I'm meant to be with.

"I'm so glad you came," I confess. "This trip wouldn't be the same without you here."

"I'm glad I did too." Eric shifts slightly, turning so he can look at me in the dim porch light. "Being here with you... it just feels right."

Before I can respond, he dips his head and kisses me, slow and unhurried, like we have all the time in the world. And for once, we actually do.

Chapter 23

I tiptoe into the kitchen of the quiet beach house and make my way to the coffee pot. It's just after seven, and the boys have been gone for at least an hour on their fishing trip.

Expecting a mostly empty pot or at least lukewarm coffee, I'm surprised to find a fresh one and a neat stack of mugs waiting. One of the girls beat me out of bed, but who?

I choose a mug, a handmade one with a ceramic mermaid on the side, fix my coffee, and head for the porch.

I stand at the railing, scanning the beach until I spot Tyler. She looks completely in her element, leggings pushed up around her calves as she wades through the shallows, searching for shells. For a moment, I consider grabbing my shoes and joining her, but I decide to let her have her quiet time. All moms deserve a little extra time to themselves. Especially on vacation.

Instead, I settle into a tall Adirondack chair and sip my coffee while I watch the waves roll in. Last night was the perfect start to our trip. We walked the shoreline, slushies in hand, spotting jellyfish and crabs, collecting shells until our pockets and purses were full. It's been too long since I've been at the beach.

When everyone went to Mexico for Avery's wedding, I was a little jealous, though I never would have admitted it out loud.

Of course, I wasn't close to Avery then, so it wouldn't have made sense for me to be invited. I lived vicariously through their pictures instead until it was my turn to put my toes in the sand. It was worth the wait.

This is the longest I've been away from Piper since she was born, and though I miss her, this time with Eric has been what my heart needed most.

"Morning," Avery groans, sliding open the balcony door and joining me. "How'd you sleep?"

"Like a baby," I start, then laugh. "No. Like a dad. We cracked the window and fell asleep listening to the waves. I could fall asleep to that sound every night."

"Same." Avery rubs her stomach. "I think I slept better last night than I have in months. Ever since we found out we were pregnant, I feel like I haven't had a full night's sleep."

"Well, you've probably been up all night worrying about raising twins," I say. "It's a lot to take in."

"What's a lot to take in?" Madison asks, stepping out with a coffee of her own. Her blonde hair falls over her satin pajama top.

"The twins," Avery explains.

Madison pulls her into a side hug. "You're going to be okay. And we'll all be here to help you."

Avery frowns. "I might have to stay home with the babies. Which means you'll have to fill Juliet's spot."

Madison waves her off. "I already assumed you wouldn't come back after the twins. I'd be happy to keep them, but honestly, paying for daycare for three kids is a lot. I have a mile-long waitlist. It won't be a problem."

Avery exhales in relief. "So you're not mad?"

"Mad? Avery, this is a dream for you. You get to raise your

babies and run your boutique, just like you wanted. I'm thrilled for you." Madison assures her.

"Hey, bums," Sierra calls, climbing the back steps towards us. "Don't tell me you just woke up."

"Maybe," I tease. "This is vacation after all. Where were you?"

"Running." She grins. "What's better than running on the beach?"

"Walking and finding treasures," Tyler answers, joining us with her woven bag. She spills her shells onto the table with a satisfied smile.

Avery raises a brow. "Tyler, didn't you used to run?"

"Back when Andrew and I were broken up for that little bit of time," Tyler says with a laugh. "Now my cardio is lifting boxes of books."

"That counts," I tell her.

"Any of you can join me for a run anytime," Sierra says, stretching. "But for now, I'm taking a shower."

Madison turns to me. "Want to grab groceries? There's a little market just down the street."

I nod. "Yes, give me ten minutes."

* * *

After our quick grocery run, we get back to the house to find the rest of the girls up and ready to explore. Breakfast is officially skipped, so instead we grab granola bars, toss them in our bags, and pile into the car bound for Tybean, the local coffee shop.

The gravel crunches beneath our tires as we pull into the lot. A salty breeze trails us up the wooden steps and inside, where we place our orders: a smoothie for Avery, because she's already had her daily coffee; a chai latte for Sierra; a vanilla cold brew for Tyler; a caramel frappe for Madison; and for me, a Red and White... cinnamon, vanilla, and espresso perfection.

Coffee in hand, we wander the row of colorful shops nearby, leaving with a handful of treasures: shell Christmas ornaments, beachy jewelry, and postcards printed with photos from a local artist.

Our next stop is Sea Side Sisters, another cheerful tourist favorite. Tyler, of course, buys a book by a local author, and the rest of us browse the booths, each of us wishing for just a little more room in our suitcases.

Finally, we head for North Beach and the Tybee Island lighthouse. We leave our drinks in the car, and make our way towards the museum, with Tyler leading the way several steps in front of us. She is already reading an informational sign when we catch up to her.

"This is Georgia's oldest and tallest lighthouse," she says, practically vibrating with excitement. "You can climb all the way to the top. The view has to be amazing."

I tilt my head back, staring up at the structure. "Yeah... I think I'll just wait down here." I wave them off. "You guys know I don't do heights."

"Oh, Ava, it's perfectly safe," Sierra says with a shrug. "Probably. I mean, they wouldn't let people climb if tons of people fell off."

I groan. "Not exactly comforting."

Tyler folds her arms. "You are going to regret it if you don't go. We'll go slow. You set the pace."

Before I can answer, Avery shakes her head. "I'm sitting this one out. My center of gravity is already weird enough. You guys climb for me and tell me if it's worth it."

I glance from the lighthouse to my friends. "It probably is pretty cool up there, huh?"

Tyler nods. "You'll be able to see for miles today. I'll even walk behind you so if you fall, you land on me."

"Not sure that would help," I mutter. "Pretty sure that just means we both die dramatically."

"You've got this," Madison says, squeezing my hand. "What is it Piper always says? I am brave. I am strong. I am nice."

That earns a small smile. "Piper is going to freak out when she hears I climbed this thing."

"Then we better get you up there so we can send her a picture," Tyler says with a grin.

We buy tickets and make our way to the lighthouse. I pause at the bottom of the narrow, spiraling staircase. "Those steps are tiny."

"Your feet aren't that big. You'll be fine." Tyler gestures me forward. "Come on."

I grip the railing and start climbing, slow and careful, sometimes touching the cool stone wall just to steady myself. At last, we emerge into the sunlight at the top, and I finally take a deep breath. The view is incredible.

"Worth it," Tyler says, already pulling out her phone to take my photo. "Get up by the rail and I'll take your picture so you can send it to Piper."

I take a cautious step back. "Nope. You can take a photo of me right here. I'll remember it without touching the rail."

"Fine," Tyler smirks, "say cheese."

* * *

Avery waves from the ground when we finally descend the metal steps that were much less intimidating on the way down. "Well?"

"You were right," I admit, glancing back at the lighthouse. "It was scary but I'll never forget that view."

Avery smiles and pulls me into a hug. "I'm so proud of you. That was a huge thing you just overcame."

I nod looking back up at the lighthouse. "Maybe sometimes it's worth facing our fears."

Madison rests a hand on my shoulder. "It's always worth it."

After the lighthouse, we head to North Beach Bar and Grill for lunch. A few too many fish tacos and one fruity drink later, we head back to the house.

When we pull into the driveway, we find the guys waiting on the porch, a bucket of beer sweating on the table between them.

"How was fishing?" Avery asks as we make our way up the steps.

"Incredible," Bryan says without hesitation. "Best money I've ever spent. We all caught enough for a feast tomorrow night."

"Great!" Madison beams. "Good job, guys."

"Looks like you ladies were out hunting and gathering too," Derek teases, nodding at our arms full of shopping bags.

"Just a few souvenirs here and there," I say with a shrug. "Check out these matching shirts we got." I pull a tie-dyed long sleeve out of the bag with the words *Tybee Island* screaming across the front in an offensively large font.

"Those are... special," Andrew laughs. "Did you get us some too?"

Tyler groans. "We didn't, but I remember where we bought

them. I'd be happy to go back."

Andrew shakes his head. "No thanks. I'll carry the memory of Derek puking off the side of the boat forever. That's the only souvenir I need."

Avery's eyes widen and she turns to her husband. "You were puking? Are you okay?"

Derek waves her off. "Just got a little seasick. I'm fine now."

Tyler frowns. "Don't you go on cruises all the time?"

"Big difference," Derek mutters. "Cruises don't rock like that. At least not often."

I glance up at Eric from where I'm tucked into the crook of his arm. "Did you have fun?"

"That's the best part," Cody jumps in before Eric can answer. "While Pukey McGee was hanging over the railing, his rod was almost bent in half. Eric grabbed it, reeled in the biggest red snapper any of us have ever seen. That fish alone is going to feed all of us tomorrow night."

"Sounds like you officially won the guys over," I say, leaning up to kiss Eric's lips.

He grins down at me. "Baby, as long as I've won you over, no one else matters.

* * *

"Okay, that was definitely not your typical ghost tour," I say as we make our way back to the cars in downtown Savannah.

"No, it wasn't, but it was so fun," Sierra gushes. "I'm not even a ghost person, but that tour was more than spooky stories. It was history and legends."

"And really good beer," Andrew adds. "Whoever came up

with the pub-crawl-slash-tour idea deserves a medal."

"Anything else anyone wants to do before we head home for the night?" Avery asks.

I shake my head. "I don't think so. We saw the fountain, walked downtown, and ate some amazing food. I'm satisfied."

"And I finally got to visit E. Shaver Booksellers, which has been on my bucket list forever," Tyler says, practically glowing.

"Nerd," Andrew teases, bumping her shoulder.

Tyler just grins.

"I just wanted to see the river walk and the cobblestone streets," Sierra says. "So, I'm good. Let's go back to the house and just hang out. We can sit on the porch, listen to the waves, and relax."

"Avery, I know you're one of the designated drivers tonight." Madison says. "Derek, you sure you're good to be the other?"

Derek nods and jingles the keys. "Yep. I promised Avery I wasn't drinking this trip, and I meant it. If she can't have a beer, I don't need one either."

Avery rolls her eyes, but she's smiling. "I told him he doesn't have to do that, but it's sweet that he did."

"You're already making enough sacrifices," Derek says, reaching over to squeeze her hand. "Let me support you the best I can."

* * *

"Ugh, this trip is exactly what I needed. Thank you so much for organizing this," I say to Madison as we walk side by side down the beach with the sound of the waves crashing in the distance.

It's our last morning here. This afternoon we'll return the rental cars and hop on a plane back to reality.

"Me too. I miss my girls, but I could stay here for a few more days," Madison says with a smile. "I'm glad you brought Eric. You two are perfect together, and it's obvious he's head over heels in love with you."

I nod. "I like him too. A lot."

Madison stops walking and turns to face me. "Girl, you more than like him. It's obvious you're just as in love with him as he is with you."

I bite my lip and shrug. "You're not wrong."

"This is a good thing. You two are perfect together. He finishes your jokes and knows what you need before you even ask. Not to mention he gave you a piggyback ride for three blocks last night because your feet hurt."

"Bryan would do the same for you."

Madison nods. "I know. Because he loves me. And I see that exact same thing between you and Eric."

"It's a lot to get used to."

Madison reaches out and squeezes my hand. "I know. But Ava, you've earned every bit of this. You're strong and capable and fiercely independent. You've proven you can do anything you set your mind to. Now it's time to let someone else do life with you."

I shake my head, staring out at the waves. "Do you know how scary that is?"

"Of course it's scary," Madison says softly. "But not everything scary is bad. Sometimes the scary parts are just the beginning of the really, really good stuff."

Chapter 24

I'm lying in bed after getting home from our trip, tossing and turning, unable to get comfortable.

How is it that I only slept next to this man for three nights and now I can't sleep alone anymore?

I pick up my phone and fire off a text.

Ava: Hopefully this doesn't wake you, but sleeping without you next to me sucks. Just thought you should know.
    Eric: Agreed. I miss you. We need to do that again soon.
    Ava: Yeah, we do. I love you. Goodnight.
    Eric: Love you too. Night.

I stare at the ceiling long after the screen goes dark, my chest heavy and restless. The bed feels too big, too quiet, too mine. By the time morning rolls around, I feel like I haven't slept at all.

"Morning!" Madison calls out in a chipper tone as she opens the door to let Piper inside for school drop-off. "Piper, your breakfast is on the table."

"Thank you!" Piper shouts, already running toward her plate.

Madison looks back at me, her brows knitting together. "Hey, no offense, but you look like crap. You okay?"

"Thanks," I say with a yawn. "I think I slept for about twenty minutes last night."

"What's wrong? You sick? Want some coffee?"

I shake my head. "No, I'm stopping at Drip on my way to the office to get something with too many espresso shots. Do you think three nights was enough to get too used to sleeping with Eric? Because I could not sleep without him last night." I groan. "That sounded pathetic."

Madison chuckles softly. "No, it didn't. I get it. After Ben moved out, I started sleeping on the couch most nights. Something about that bed felt too big and too empty. The couch made me feel less... vulnerable, I guess. I still do it sometimes."

I frown and lower my voice. "So, my options are sleep on the couch or ask Eric to move in with me."

Madison smirks and glances toward Carson, who's sitting at the table eating scrambled eggs and chatting with Piper. "I'd go with option two."

"Isn't it too soon? We've only been dating for, what, four months?"

Madison shrugs. "How long do you want to go without sleeping?"

I roll my eyes.

"I'm just saying," she continues. "If my divorce papers didn't say Bryan and I couldn't live together before marriage, we'd already be there."

I sigh. "Maybe I'll talk to him and see what he thinks."

By the time Madison and I finish talking, my mind is a blur of what-ifs. I promise myself I'll bring it up with Eric soon. When the timing feels right, and when I'm not running on caffeine and nerves.

* * *

Saturday comes quicker than I expect.

"Mom, hurry!" Piper calls out as she races ahead of me toward the park.

It's the Saturday following our trip to Georgia, and today Piper and I are soaking up every second we can together. We have been to Tyler's bookstore for story time. Then we grabbed lunch at Rio Escondido and drinks from Drip. Now I'm carrying Piper's cup full of chocolate milk and whipped cream in one hand, with my mocha latte in the other as we make our way to the park. The weather in Kansas at this time of year is all over the place, so we decided to take advantage of the seventy-degree weather while we could, so we are walking to the park from downtown.

"Do not cross the street without me," I warn Piper as she reaches the intersection and pauses.

She furrows her brow. "I know. I wouldn't do that," her face full of disgust at me for even suggesting she would.

"I know. I'm sorry," I tell her as I close the distance. "You just kinda looked like you were so excited you might have run into the street without thinking."

"I'm smarter than that," Piper mutters with a scowl as she takes my hand and we begin to cross the street. "Oh look. Carson is here!" she says, perking up and pointing toward the park.

I squint and follow her gesture to find Carson, Eric, and a woman sitting in the shade under a tree on a blanket. They're laughing, relaxed, a picture-perfect little family. My steps slow, then stop altogether.

The woman turns her head, and my stomach drops. I know that face. I've seen it in tagged photos, in the deep scroll of my late-night social media stalking sessions.

Briana. Carson's mom.

Of course it's her. And judging by the smile she flashes in my direction, she knows exactly what she's doing. She shifts closer to Eric, resting her head lightly on his shoulder as if she belongs there, as if she always has.

The air leaves my lungs in one sharp breath. My heart races, my stomach twists, and all I can think is how stupid I've been. I was going to ask him to move in. I thought we were building something real. And yet here he is, sitting under a tree with his ex and their son, looking like the family I'll never be part of. His ex that he lead me to believe was totally out of the picture.

"Come on, Mom," Piper says, tugging at my hand. "Let's go say hi."

I shake my head and force a smile that doesn't reach my eyes. "Baby, we can't. We have to go home."

Her little brow furrows. "But I wanted to play at the park."

"I know, kiddo. I'm sorry. I feel like I'm going to throw up. I need to go home and lie down. We can come back another time." I say, picking her up and seating her on my hip as though she weighs nothing.

Piper reaches up to touch my forehead as I have done to her countless times. "You don't have a fever," she says.

"Good. Maybe it will pass soon then. I just need to lie down, okay?"

Piper nods and rests her head on my shoulder as we finish our walk to the car. "I hope you feel better soon, Mommy."

"Me too, baby. Me too."

Once we are home, I get Piper settled in the living room with a movie and then make my way upstairs. Once I am changed into my holiest sweats and baggiest T-shirt, I crawl under my covers and finally allow the tears to fall.

How could he have done this to me? It was so hard to let him in, to let my guard down. And for what? For him to be with her? Without even telling me?

I was going to ask him to move in with me. Now all I want is to forget he even exists.

I settle into my bed and after a good cry, I fall into a deep sleep for the first time since the last night I slept with Eric beside me.

I don't know how long I sleep, but when I finally drift off, it's deep and dreamless. The kind of sleep that comes only after your body gives up on your heart. The sound of the doorbell drags me out of it, my head pounding, eyes swollen.

In my half-asleep stupor, I pick up my phone and open the app. There on my porch stands Carson and Eric.

I hit the answer button. "Hey."

He leans forward with that classic smile. "Hey. We're here for dinner."

Dinner. Shit.

I forgot I invited them to dinner tonight. The kids were going to watch a movie and I was finally going to get the nerve to ask Eric about moving in. Obviously that won't be happening now. Not when he spent his day playing happy family with his ex-girlfriend and didn't even bother to tell me about it.

For a second, I consider turning him away. But instead, Piper, being the helpful child that she is, opens the door and lets them inside. I have got to talk to that kid about not answering the door without my permission.

I crawl out of bed and make my way downstairs, still wearing my most unattractive outfit. I guess if I'm going to get dumped, or maybe do the dumping, it doesn't matter how I look for him anymore.

Eric's face softens as he sees me make my way down the staircase. "Ava, are you okay?"

I shake my head. "No."

"She's very sick," Piper tells him.

"Oh, no. What can I do?" Eric asks, moving towards me to lay his hand on my forehead.

I lean back quickly to avoid his touch.

"She doesn't have a fever. I already checked." Piper reports, not moving her eyes from the television.

"Why didn't you call me? I could have brought you soup or medicine." Eric says, with a face still full of concern.

"You were at the park so you were busy," Piper reports, still without moving her head.

So much for not telling him what I saw.

He furrows his brows. "The park?"

Piper nods. "Yeah, we saw you there."

"My mom was there." Carson offers.

"I saw. That was a fun surprise," I say, landing my eyes on Eric.

"Yep. She brought me a toy." Carson says, proudly holding up the stuffed dog he's been holding since they walked in.

"That was really nice of her." I tell him, before turning to look at Eric. "We should probably talk." I say, motioning towards upstairs where at least we can argue with the door closed.

Eric nods. "Yeah. We should. Kids, stay down here, we're going to go upstairs. We will be right back."

I lead Eric up the wooden staircase into my bedroom and close the door behind him. He takes a seat on the bed and pats the spot next to him. Instead, I stay standing, keeping distance between us.

"You're not sick, are you? You're mad at me." Eric says.

"Good job, detective." I mutter with a scowl.

"What... what did I do?"

I throw my arms open wide. "How's Briana? You three looked awfully cozy at the park with her head resting on your shoulder. What a cute little family. Almost like you didn't just spend last weekend with your girlfriend on vacation with all of her friends."

Eric stands slowly, brow furrowed and hands raised slightly, like he's carefully approaching a wounded animal. "Ava, that wasn't what it looked like."

I cross my arms in front of my chest, as though it'll help hold me together. "It looked like you were playing house with your ex. The ex you told me wasn't even in the picture. I feel like I missed a whole chapter here."

He runs his hand through his hair. "We were playing at the park and she just showed up unannounced. I didn't know she was in town. One minute, I'm pushing him on the swings and the next minute she's making her way across the park introducing herself to him as his mom. I didn't know what to do. So we let her sit down with us and she gave him a toy."

"And then you let her stake her claim to you right in front of the entire town."

"Do you think I wanted her touching me? No. As soon as she laid on my shoulder, I got up and put distance between the two of us. I was just trying to keep things calm for Carson. He deserves that much. The kid didn't even remember what she looked like until she showed up today."

I nod, fighting back tears. As much as I want to stay mad and not believe him, I can't. I know he loves his son. I know he would do anything to protect him, and I know he's a good man.

"Why didn't you call or text me?" I ask. "Fawn Creek is a small town. If I didn't see it myself, someone else was bound to see it and let me know. Do you know how embarrassing that would have been?"

He exhales and shakes his head, looking across the room out the bedroom window. "I don't know. I should have. But I panicked. There's nothing in the single dad handbook about how to handle your kid's estranged mother when she randomly shows up out of nowhere." He shakes his head. "Do you know why she showed up here today? Not because she missed her son. It was because she saw pictures on Avery's Instagram of all of us at the beach. She didn't want her kid back. She came back because I'm finally happy and it pissed her off. Obviously, she came to try to ruin things and it worked."

I pause, staring at him in disbelief. Not because I don't believe him, but because I'm shocked that this woman is an even bigger monster than I realized. "Seriously?"

He nods. "Ava, nothing she could ever do or say will make me want her back. Carson means the world to me, and the fact that she could just walk away from him is still something I can't wrap my head around. She's not getting back into his life if I have any say over it, and she will never get back into mine."

I let out a breath. Somehow, my heart feels even more broken than it did a couple of hours ago. But now for different reasons.

"Eric, I'm sorry for jumping to conclusions. I saw her, and the way she looked at me just broke me," I admit. "It's taken me a long time to move forward with my life and to love again. I was going to ask if you and Carson wanted to move in with us. And I think a part of me was bracing for it all to fall apart."

Eric raises a brow. "You were going to ask me to move in?"

I nod. "Well, I was trying to get the nerve to do it. I've been working on it all week, rehearsing it while I was driving, imagining every possible way it could go. And then this happened. Maybe I'm not ready after all."

Eric picks up my hand and pulls me toward him. He sits down on the bed and guides me into his lap.

"Ava, I love you. And I promise I'm going to show you how much you mean to me. I'm not going anywhere, and I'm not going to be with anyone else. I love you."

"I love you too."

"Then don't worry," he says softly. "I'll prove to you that you can trust me. And when you're really ready, Carson and I will happily pack our bags and move in."

* * *

"So, she just showed up with no warning after being completely absent in that kid's life? All because of an Instagram post?" Sierra shakes her head in disbelief. We are back on my porch for our Sunday night Wine Down, and we are rehashing my weekend, and this time Sierra came into town to join us. "I'm not a fighter, but I'd love to kick that woman's ass."

"Same," I agree. "You should have seen the way she looked at me. All smug, like she had somehow won."

"Well, I can definitely see how that would upset you. After you had finally decided to trust this guy with your whole heart. But I can assure you Eric is in no danger of getting back together with that woman," Sierra assures me. "I saw that way he was looking at you at the beach. He's all yours."

"I know that," I say quickly. "I really do. But in the moment

196

all I could think about was my heart breaking."

Madison reaches over and gives my hand a quick squeeze. "That's normal. She showed up out of nowhere and stirred things up. Of course you reacted."

"Yeah, but I don't like how I reacted," I admit. "I thought I was past this whole doubting-everything stage, and then one look from her had me spiraling. It felt... weak."

Sierra shrugs. "You're human, not weak. The important part is you didn't let it ruin things between you and Eric."

I nod, but the guilt is still there. "We're good now, but I think I need to slow down just a little. That whole conversation we had about moving in together... I think I panicked. I want it, but I want to be sure I'm not doing it just because I'm scared of losing him."

Madison frowns. "I hate that you're second-guessing yourself, but I get it. You have to do what feels right, especially with Piper and Carson to think about."

"Exactly. I just want to know I'm doing it for the right reasons."

Sierra tips her wine glass toward me. "Well, that's what this is for. Time to sit, think, and get your head straight. And if she shows up again, we'll all be ready to fight her off for you."

That makes me laugh, which feels like a relief after the heaviness of the weekend. "Thanks. I hope next time I won't let her knock me so far off balance."

Chapter 25

Once my friends leave, it's time for Piper and I to get ready for the week ahead of us.

"Pipes! Shower time!" I call up the staircase to her where she is playing in her room.

"Ugh. Okay," she groans back. "Do I have to wash my hair?"

"Yes!"

"Why?"

"Because I let you skip it last night. Just go shower, please!" I call up from the bottom of the stairs.

"Fine."

I hear the stomp of her feet toward the bathroom. Good enough for me.

With the bedtime routine in motion, I turn back to the kitchen and start my own nightly checklist... load the dishwasher, set the coffee pot for tomorrow, pack Piper's lunch. I'm cutting her Nutella sandwich into a circle when my phone starts to ring.

It's Emilee.

Hitting the speakerphone button, I answer, still working on the sandwich. "What's up?"

"Ava?" The panic in her voice is clear. "My water broke. Mom and Dad are in Owen on a date night. Any chance you can keep Jacob until they get back?"

I wipe my hands on a paper towel. "Yes, of course. Want me to come get him?"

"We'll just drop him off if that's okay. We're getting ready to head to the car now."

"Yes, perfect. Send his school stuff and I'll keep him overnight. He can go with Piper in the morning."

"Are you sure?"

"Very sure. You just focus on having that baby. I'll be on the porch waiting for you."

When we hang up, I race upstairs to give Piper a heads-up about the sleepover, then dash back down just in time to see Emilee and Adam's white SUV pull into the drive.

After they go through a quick round of hugs and kisses, I take his overnight bag and backpack, wish them luck, and step inside just as Piper comes barreling down the stairs.

"Yay! Sleepover!" she cheers. "Can we sleep downstairs tonight?"

"Yes."

"Can we stay up late watching a movie?"

I shake my head. "Tomorrow's a school day. But you can start one now and maybe finish before bed. Deal?"

"Yay!" both kids cheer.

"Okay, Piper, let Jacob pick the movie. I'll grab blankets and make you a pallet on the floor."

It's just after ten when I finish my shower, and check my messages from Emilee. *No baby yet.* With the house finally quiet, I wander down the hall, checking lights and doors before stopping outside the guest room.

When we moved in here, I worked hard on this space. I wanted it to feel warm and inviting, and available to anyone that might come to visit. Honestly though, it's only been used once, when Madison's girls came over to stay the night and Piper suggested the three of them take over the spare room. The three girls fit just right in the queen sized bed, all jumbled together in my pile of throw pillows.

Perhaps this room wasn't meant for guests after all. Maybe it's meant for Carson and it's time to start emptying this space, getting it ready for him. I'm already daydreaming about paint colors and themes when I hear soft sniffles drifting up the stairs from the living room.

I make my way down the stairs and tiptoe to the makeshift bed, crouching beside Jacob. "Hey, buddy. You okay?"

He nods but keeps sniffling, his little chest rising and falling with uneven breaths.

"Miss your mama?" I ask gently.

Another nod, his bottom lip sticking out.

"I'm sorry, buddy. I know she misses you too. It's hard to be away from our moms, huh?"

"Yeah," he whispers, giving another sniffle.

"Well, I can't make her come back any faster, but what if we turn on a cartoon? Think that might help you fall asleep?"

He nods again. "I like to go to sleep to Bluey."

"I love Bluey." I grab the remote and find an episode. "Can I watch with you for a little bit?"

When he nods, I hurry upstairs for my phone in case Emilee texts, then curl up on the couch. Before the first episode even ends, Jacob's breathing has evened out and he's sound asleep.

I switch off the TV, plug in my phone, and settle deeper into the couch just in case he wakes up scared in the night. Thankfully, we all sleep soundly until morning.

* * *

"Good morning, beautiful!" Cassidy calls from behind the counter at Drip as soon as I walk in after dropping the kids off at school.

"Hey!" I grin back at her. "Can I get a large vanilla latte with an extra shot? Oh, and can you add some cinnamon too?"

"Sure! That sounds like a fun combination." She taps the order into the register.

"I had it when we were on Tybee, and I've been thinking about it ever since," I confess. "On the way here, I realized it was something you could easily make."

"Of course. I'll make anything as long as I have the ingredients. And if I don't, I can usually get them."

"You're the best." I slide my card across the counter, but before I can put it away, my phone chimes. I freeze, digging for it, but it's only an email.

"Damn. No baby yet," I mutter.

"Who's having a baby? It's too early for Avery," Cassidy calls over the hiss of the espresso machine.

"Emilee. Zach's sister. Her water broke last night, so I kept Jacob overnight and took him to school this morning. I was hoping I'd have some news by now. That's a long time to be in labor."

"Oh, I hope you hear something soon." Cassidy nods, setting my latte on the counter. "I'll be praying for her. I can't wait to see pictures."

"Me neither. Thank you! Have a good day."

I grab my coffee and head toward the office, texting Emilee on the way.

Ava: Jacob made it to school safe and sound this morning. Let me know if you need me to pick him up afterward or if I can

do anything else for you.

Emilee: Thank you! You are a lifesaver. If you could go ahead and plan to get him after school, that would be great. I'm progressing but slowly.

Ava: Not a problem at all. Sending you lots of baby dust today. I can't wait to see him. Get lots of rest and don't worry about a thing here.

Emilee: Will do. Thank you!

The rest of the day flies by as I get lost in updating listings, answering emails, and returning phone calls. Before I know it, the day is over and it's time to pick up the kids.

I'm just pulling up to the school when a notification from my doorbell camera pops up. When I tap it, Eric's face fills the screen, grinning.

"Knock, knock," he says dramatically.

I hit the microphone button and play along. "Who's there?"

"Olive."

"Olive who?"

"Olive you... even though you order far too much from Amazon."

I groan, but a smile tugs at my lips. "It's called job security."

"You're right. Thank you for your contribution."

I laugh and shake my head. "Don't worry, there's plenty more where that came from."

"I have no doubts," he says with a grin. "Any baby news yet?"

"Nothing," I groan. "I'm trying so hard not to bother her, but the suspense is killing me."

"Patience, grasshopper. I better get back to my route. Let me know when you hear something. I love you."

"I will. I love you too."

I close the app and slide my phone into my pocket. Just as I step onto the lawn of the school, my phone buzzes again. This time it's Emilee. When I open my messages, a photo pops up, and I stop in my tracks. One of the sweetest, squishiest newborns I've ever seen fills the screen.

Emilee: Meet Zachery Lane Reeves. He's here and he's perfect. Mom and baby are doing good.

I smile, reading the name again and letting it settle in my chest. Before I can reply, another text comes through.

Emilee: Hope you don't mind me naming him after my brother. Do you mind showing Jacob when he gets out of school? Mom is here with me and can come get him from you in a little bit.

Ava: Of course I don't mind. Tell your mom to stay as late as she wants. I can keep him another night if needed.

Emilee: It's okay. She's going to bring him to see me before visiting hours are over. I miss him.

Ava: He misses you, too. He's going to be so excited to see his baby brother. I can't wait to snuggle him myself once you guys are home and settled.

Emilee: Thanks again for your help. We love you.

Ava: Love you too. Get some rest while you can. You're going to need it.

* * *

"Hey," Adam says, meeting me at the door. "Come on in.

Emilee will be glad to see you."

It's been two days since she called from the hospital. Last night, she texted to say they were heading home, and I knew I had to do something to show her a little love after her hospital stay.

"Oh good. I don't want to interrupt anything. I just wanted to drop off some food for dinner," I tell him, following him into the kitchen. I set the casserole dish on the counter and begin unloading the rest of the bags into the fridge.

"Hey, you." Emilee's voice is soft and groggy behind me. When I turn, she looks exactly how she sounds... exhausted.

"Hey. What are you doing up walking around? You just had a baby," I tease. "I'm just dropping off some dinner and then I'll be out of your hair."

She smiles softly. "You didn't have to do that."

"I know. I wanted to take a little pressure off so you can just spend time together as a family. I brought chicken enchiladas. You can eat them now or freeze them. There's also cut-up fruit, cottage cheese, a loaf of sourdough, and gelato for dessert."

"That sounds amazing. Thank you, really." Her voice wavers. "Want to come meet Baby Zach?"

For a second, I pause. It's still strange hearing that name, but I know I'll adjust.

"Yes, of course. If you're ready for him to meet visitors."

"You aren't a visitor. You're his Aunt Ava. You and Piper are our family, and I'm sorry it took me so long to realize that." Her eyes glisten. "I hate to think of everything I missed because I was angry at the world when I lost Zach."

I move toward her and pull her into a hug. "Em, it's okay. You were young, and so was I. We handled it the best we knew how. What matters now is that we have each other."

After washing my hands, I settle on the sofa and wait while Adam carefully lowers the tiny bundle of blue into my arms. The moment his weight settles against me, my heart squeezes. He scrunches himself up tight, lets out a little sigh, and smacks his lips in his sleep.

"Emilee, he's perfect," I whisper. "Even more perfect than the pictures you sent. And he's so tiny and squishy. I love him already."

"Mom said he looks like Piper did as a baby," Emilee says.

"He really does. Same nose, same little dimple on his chin." My throat tightens. "I miss her being this little. I miss that baby stage."

"You can come over and snuggle him anytime you want," she says.

"And call me if you need a break. Even if it's just someone to hold him while you shower. My business is finally organized enough that I can drop things and come running if you need me."

Emilee perks up. "So your assistant is doing a good job?"

"She's amazing. She's coming three days a week now and keeping my office running. Next year she'll be a senior, so she'll only be in school half days, and I plan to teach her more of the business side. I really think she might be my first agent someday. I'm excited to teach her the ropes, like Jessica taught me."

"You're going to be an incredible mentor. She's lucky to have you. And so are we."

I cradle Zach in my arms, his tiny fingers curling around mine, and let the quiet settle around us. These are the moments that really count... the tiny blips of time in a day where we find ourselves connecting with the people we love. That's what matters.

Time doesn't stop for anyone, whether we think we're ready or not. Maybe I need to focus less on worrying about being ready to take the next step with Eric. If I wait too long, I'll miss too much.

I take a slow breath, breathing in the sweet smell of the newborn in my arms and realize that maybe being ready isn't about having everything figured out. Maybe it's about stepping forward, one small, scared, and hopeful moment at a time.

And right now, holding this new life in my arms, I feel like I can do just that.

Chapter 26

"Happy Valentine's Day," I say as I step through the door of Sierra's salon, holding an iced coffee for each of us. I just delivered one to Tyler downstairs, too.

"Oh, you're officially my favorite Valentine," Sierra says, taking her drink. "Do you have any romantic plans today?"

"Nope. Unless you count being homeroom mom for Piper's classroom party. If Piper's classmates are anything like her, they think Valentine's Day is totally cringe." I shake my head. "But Eric and Carson are coming over for dinner tonight."

"Have you talked to him about moving in yet?" Sierra asks, sipping her drink.

"Not yet, but I'm going to. I'm just waiting for his Valentine's gift to arrive. Hopefully it shows up today like it's supposed to. Then, I'll do it. What about you guys? Doing anything special?"

Sierra plops down in a chair and flips on her hair straightener. "We're doing a double date at home with Tyler and Andrew. We ordered a pan of street tacos that are supposed to be arranged in the shape of a heart, and Tyler is making us a pitcher of margaritas. I think the boys are planning a fire in the fire pit. They are always looking for an excuse to set something on fire."

I laugh. "Typical country boys. Sounds like you have a great night ahead of you."

Just then the elevator dings. I peek into the hallway just as the painfully slow doors slide open to reveal Beth from Fawn Creek Floral, her arms loaded with two arrangements.

"Sheesh, I thought I was saving myself some energy taking the elevator instead of the stairs. That has to be the slowest elevator I've ever been in."

"Here, let me help." I leave my coffee on the table outside Sierra's door to take one of the arrangements.

"Ava, yours is the one with red and white roses," Beth says, handing it to me. "Sierra, you have the one with the sunflowers."

I thank her and carry mine into my office, setting it just inside the door.

"Now, don't think it's lost on me that I just delivered the delivery man's flowers," Beth teases. "That boy has it bad for you, Ava. He ordered those the first weekend of January. First Valentine's order I got by weeks."

"She has it just as bad," Sierra says with a grin. "I bet Cody ordered yesterday."

Beth laughs. "It's the thought that counts. Okay girls, I have a lot of deliveries to make. Happy Valentine's Day!"

"You too!" we call as she heads down the stairs.

"Alright," I tell Sierra, "I better go knock out my to-do list while I can."

I fire off a quick text to thank Eric for the flowers and wish him a Happy Valentine's Day before diving into work. The morning flies by, and soon I'm on the way to Piper's school for her Valentine's party.

Just as I put my car in park at the curb, my phone buzzes with the notification I've been waiting for. I open the app and Eric's face fills my screen.

"Hey, just your friendly neighborhood delivery man stopping by to leave love and a little cardboard at your doorstep."

I grin and press the microphone button. "Glad I caught you. I need you to open that box."

He raises a brow. "That's a new request. What is it?"

"Your Valentine's Day gift."

He shakes the package and scowls. "This feels too heavy to be lingerie."

I roll my eyes. "Just open it."

My heart pounds as he slices the tape with his pocketknife.

"It's a... doormat?"

"Read it."

"Welcome... The Garrison/Montgomery Family." He looks back at the screen, stunned. "You got me a doormat with our names on it?"

"I got *us* a doormat with our names on it," I say, my stomach fluttering. "If you and Carson are ready to move in with me and Piper... well, that is."

I bite my lip, half-expecting him to laugh or protest.

Eric's grin is immediate and wide. "More than ready."

"Then let's do it," I say, smiling so hard my cheeks ache. "Happy Valentine's Day."

I set my phone down, heart still fluttering, and take a deep breath. Today really is shaping up to be perfect.

* * *

"Okay, boys and girls. Let's finish up our yummy snacks that Piper brought for us, and then we'll play Bingo until it's time to pack up and go home," Mrs. Blum announces before turning to me. "Ava, thank you so much for all the effort you put into today's party. The snacks were delicious... especially the do-it-yourself chocolate-covered strawberry station. Honestly, when you told me your idea, I was afraid it was going to be pure chocolate chaos, but the kids really enjoyed it."

"I'm so glad it went well. It definitely could have gone sideways," I admit. "I think letting each kid have their own bowl of chocolate and toppings at their desk saved us."

Mrs. Blum laughs. "Agreed. And it was time-consuming enough to count as a craft project. That's a win for sure."

I look around at the classroom full of chocolate-mouthed first graders, my daughter included, who is currently licking the inside of her dipping bowl like she hasn't eaten in days. "I can't believe the school year is almost over and this is the last party of the year. Being homeroom mom has been so much fun."

"Well, we were lucky to have you. I know you're busy, but Piper was always so excited to announce how many days were left until her mom came to school again. Parents don't realize how much these kids love seeing them here. I know not everyone can do it, but it's so special when it happens."

I nod, feeling a lump rise in my throat. "I love it, too. I like being able to pop in for things like this. It's one of the reasons I love my job. For the most part, I can schedule my life around moments like these."

Mrs. Blum smiles. "You know, when I told you at the start of the school year how proud Zach would be of you, I had no idea how true that would turn out to be. You're doing a great job, Ava. I'm proud of you."

Her words hit harder than I expect. Proud. That's what I want Piper to feel about me. Honestly, it's how I want to feel about myself, too.

And for the first time in a long time, I really do.

* * *

"Mmmm... I love heart-shaped pizza," Carson says, taking a bite and letting the melted cheese drip down his chin.

"Does it taste any different than circle pizza?" Eric asks.

"Yes. It tastes like love," Carson replies, working to swallow his mouthful of food.

I laugh and glance at Eric. The table is a mess of crumbs and melted cheese... the kind of chaos that only happens when everyone's happy. "I can confirm that it was made with love. Especially that sourdough pizza crust. Not too bad for my first try."

"It was incredible. You've ruined regular pizza for me forever," he says, leaning back in his chair with a grin.

"Well, lucky for you, I enjoy cooking for the people I love." My gaze drifts between him and Carson, then to Piper, who is already reaching for her second slice. "And I love you all so much."

Eric's expression softens, and he reaches across the table for my hand. "We love you too."

"I know you do," I tell him with a smirk before turning toward the kids. "Do you think we should tell them the big news?"

Piper's eyes widen. "Wait! Let me guess. I'm finally getting a sea otter."

I blink. "What? No."

Piper frowns. "Darn it. I thought the city changed their mind and decided I could have one for a pet after all."

I shake my head. "Sorry, kid. It's still against city code to

211

have a wild marine animal as a pet."

"But," Eric interjects, "we do have some news that's almost as good. Piper, what do you think about me and Carson moving in with you and your mom?"

Piper springs from her chair, nearly knocking it over. "What! Really?"

"Really," I confirm. "Carson can have the spare room next to Piper's."

"Can we paint the walls?" Carson pleads.

"Of course, any color you want," I tell him.

"Even Minecraft creeper green?" he asks.

"If that's what'll make you happy," Eric smiles, reaching across the table to squeeze my hand.

"And a garden in the backyard?" Carson suggests.

"With strawberries and giant sunflowers!" Piper adds, bouncing in her seat.

"Absolutely," I agree, laughing. "As long as I'm not the one in charge of keeping the plants alive."

Eric chuckles. "I can take that duty. Someone's got to water them."

"Deal!" Carson says, pumping his little fists.

Piper leans across the table, eyes sparkling. "I can't wait for all of my favorite people to live in my house!"

Chapter 27

"It's the big day!" Cassidy calls to Avery as she walks into the coffee shop with Derek and Juliet. "How are you feeling?"

"Nervous, excited, exhilarated," Avery lists. "I just can't wait for this to be over and start the next chapter of our lives."

"So, who all is coming to the adoption hearing?" I ask from where I stand near the counter.

"Everyone," Derek says. "Both our parents, Tyler, Andrew, Madison, Bryan, Cody, Sierra..."

"Me!" Cassidy chimes in. "Devin will be here any minute to cover for me so I can come with you."

"So basically all of Fawn Creek," I say.

"Pretty much," Avery shrugs. "Babe, can you pass out the shirts? They're all labeled."

"Oh yeah." Derek sets the tote bag he's carrying on a table and digs around inside, handing shirts to me and Cassidy. I unroll mine and read it aloud.

"Adoption Squad. I love it."

Derek unzips his jacket to reveal his matching shirt. "She's the only one I will ever willingly wear pink for."

"I don't know," Bryan says as he joins us with Madison in tow. He's layered a black long sleeve under his pink T-shirt. "I think it brings out your eyes. It really goes with your skin tone."

"Thanks, buddy," Derek says, shaking his head.

Avery comes back with a coffee and takes a sip.

"Um, should you be drinking caffeine?" Bryan asks.

"I drink it for your protection, buddy," Avery scowls.

Bryan holds his hands up. "I'm just saying, I thought that wasn't good for babies."

"My doctor said one cup a day is fine. This is my one cup," Avery explains.

"But did it say 8 ounces, 12, or 16?" Bryan asks.

"It's a small. Totally fine."

"You probably need to watch out for yourself," Madison warns him. "She might kill you in the middle of the coffee shop."

Bryan scoops Juliet into his arms. "You wouldn't hit a man with a baby in your arms, would you?"

"No blood on the floor, please," Cassidy says, laughing.

Avery shakes her head and checks her watch. "We better get going. Everyone else should be meeting us there. And don't worry Bryan, I'll get you, one day."

* * *

An hour later, we're seated in a courtroom that smells faintly of polished wood and coffee from the vending machine near the back. Judge Morrison pauses, looks around the room, and then back at the paperwork in front of her. She turns to Avery, Derek, and Juliet with a soft smile.

"I've reviewed the petition for adoption, and based on the crowd we have gathered here today, it is very clear that Miss Juliet is a very loved and special little girl."

"Yes, Your Honor," Avery says, nodding and reaching down to squeeze Juliet's hand. Juliet looks up at Avery and then Derek, offering a shy smile while gripping the hem of her Adoption Squad shirt. Her sequin headband sparkles under the bright lights of the courtroom.

"Do you understand," the judge continues, now looking at Derek, "that by signing this order, you are accepting all legal responsibilities for this child as your daughter? And furthermore, she is yours in every way that the law can make her?"

Derek speaks clearly and confidently. "Yes, Your Honor."

Avery lets out a heavy sigh, the weight of the moment settling over her. Even from my seat, I can see the tears brimming in her eyes. I blink quickly to fight mine back, but one slips down anyway.

The judge nods slowly. "Then it is my honor and privilege to grant this adoption. From this day forward, Juliet is legally and forever your daughter."

* * *

"Okay, everyone ready?" the photographer, Kari, calls from the edge of the street.

Juliet's entire Adoption Squad is standing on the steps of the county courthouse as we pose for a group photo. Once the photos are taken and we're given permission to move, I turn to Avery and pull her into a hug.

"Congratulations, you guys. Thank you so much for letting me be part of your big day."

"I'm so glad you could come," she whispers into my ear.

"Avery, it was genius to hire a photographer for this," Tyler says as she steps forward for her turn to hug her best friend.

"Well, we're making it multi-purpose," Avery admits. "After this, we're going to do some family photos and a few maternity shots. I want to get a few before I end up on bed rest."

"Is that a possibility?" I ask, raising a brow.

"Nothing official yet, but since we're having twins, it's highly likely. Even more likely that they'll be early. I just want to be prepared. We only have about six weeks left."

"Good idea," Tyler nods. "Which means we need to get moving on your shower too. I'll get back to you with a date later today. Then, when we get back from vacation I'll get to work on planning."

"Oh, where are you going?" I ask.

"Back to Georgia," Tyler says with an excited clap. "I can't wait to show Molly the beach and play in the sand with her. Tybee Island might actually be my happy place."

"And wherever she's happy and can take a break from stressing about work is my happy place too," Andrew adds, pulling her close.

"We created a monster," Madison jokes, shaking her head at Bryan.

"And I'm so glad you did," Tyler laughs.

I look around and back at my friends. "Well girls, I'm going to head out. I have a paint order ready for pickup at the hardware store."

"Oh, what are we painting?" Tyler asks.

"Carson's new bedroom," I tell her.

"So, it's really happening then." Madison grins.

"Yes! This weekend actually, so I want his room painted and ready."

I hug everyone one last time, my heart still full from watching

Juliet become officially part of her family.

The air outside feels crisp, and I can't help smiling at the thought of what's waiting at home. Carson's room is just a blank canvas now, but by the end of the weekend it'll be his space. A place for him to feel at home, safe, and happy. I slip my keys from my pocket and take a deep breath, imagining what life will be like by this time next week. But, today, it's all about making that little room feel like it's always belonged to him, and I can't wait to get started.

* * *

"Mom, thanks again for keeping the kids for us. Unloading the U-Haul will go so much faster without two kids underfoot," I tell her. "Need anything before I go?"

My mom waves me off. "Nope, we'll be just fine. I have a full day planned with these two, so feel free to take all the time you need." She stands from the sofa and heads toward the kitchen. "Now, tell the kids bye so we can go make some cookies."

"Cookies!" Piper and Carson shout in unison.

They run over to hug me goodbye before racing off to join my mom in the kitchen. Carson has taken to her just as quickly as I hoped, and I can't wait to hear all about their day.

By the time I make it back to the house, Eric is already backing the U-Haul into the driveway. I park my SUV at the street, carry my things inside, and meet him back in the driveway.

"You ready for this? Final chance to back out," Eric says with a grin, greeting me with a kiss.

"There's no chance I'm backing out. Carson's room is already painted bright green with a giant creeper face stenciled on the wall," I laugh. "I can't wait for him to see it when he gets home."

Eric smirks. "He's going to love it. Let's get all of this stuff into the garage, then we'll start on his room first."

We work diligently, moving boxes and organizing them by room. In no time, the garage is completely full. I step back and survey our progress.

"You have a lot of boxes labeled miscellaneous," I observe. "And I had no idea you owned so many deer mounts," I add with a wince.

Eric blinks. "I told you I'm a hunter."

I nod. "You did. I guess I didn't realize you were this deep into it."

"I could take the mounts back to my parents' house," he offers.

I shake my head and move toward him, wrapping my arms around his waist. I look up at him. "No, of course not. You live here now, and that means so do your stuffed animals. We'll just have to find a place for them. And I'll have to get used to them staring at me."

Eric smirks. "How about the garage? They can stay in the corner with my weight bench. You'll only ever see them if you need to park the car in here."

"Are you sure you don't mind? I want you to feel just as at home here as I do."

Eric pulls me close, kissing my forehead. "Babe, anywhere I'm with you feels like home. The rest is just stuff."

I look up and kiss his lips again. "I love you."

"I love you, too," he grins. "Let's go return the rental truck and grab some lunch, then come home and get all this put away. What do you think?"

"I think it sounds like you read my mind."

* * *

"Okay, Carson, close your eyes," I command, standing in front of his bedroom door.

Carson giggles and squeezes his eyes tightly shut. "Ready!"

"Okay." Eric leads us in a countdown. "3...2...1!"

I fling open the door, and Carson's eyes snap open.

"Woah!" he shouts, barreling inside. "You painted it green just like I wanted! And there's a big creeper face on the wall! This is the coolest room in the entire world!"

He dives onto the bed, snuggling into the Minecraft bedding he and Eric brought from the last house. "I love it!"

I sit on the edge of the bed, heart swelling. "I'm so glad. All your toys are here, and we can move things around if you want."

Carson beams at me, then wraps his arms around my waist in a tight hug. My chest tightens with warmth, a happy ache spreading through me. This is exactly what I hoped for... Carson feeling safe and at home here.

Meanwhile, Piper and Carson make a beeline for the Lego table under the window, pulling out the clear totes of colorful blocks. The room quickly fills with the familiar clatter of bricks and laughter, and I watch, smiling.

"I don't know who loves this room more. You or Carson," Eric teases as he sits next to me on the bed. "You did a great job."

I smile proudly. "It was a lot of fun. I wanted to give him a space he would enjoy."

"And you nailed it." Eric squeezes my hand. "Thank you for putting that kind of work into making my kid feel at home."

I rest my head on his shoulder. "I love him. He deserves this.

You both do."

Carson looks up at me from the floor, then jumps into my arms. "Thank you for my new room. I love it and I love you."

The sound of him saying those words makes my chest tighten. "I love you too, Buddy," I whisper, and he dashes back to Piper, oblivious to the tears forming in my eyes.

In this moment, everything in the world is right.

Chapter 28

"Hey! How was the beach?" I ask Tyler as I walk into Madison's daycare. It's the Monday following her trip, and she is here dropping Molly off.

Tyler groans and shakes her head. "Great. Until it wasn't."

"Oh no."

"Yeah, the first night was perfect. Then I woke up the next morning puking my guts up. I tried to power through and enjoy playing at the beach with Molly, but after a couple of hours, I couldn't take much more and had to go inside and lie down. I ended up on the couch with a sleeve of saltine crackers and a two-liter of Sprite for most of the day."

I step back, as though Tyler might still be contagious.

She shakes her head. "No, I don't feel bad anymore, don't worry. We were able to do a little bit of exploring on Saturday and I never got sick again, but I think all the puking on Friday just whooped me."

Madison looks up from where she is sitting on the floor with Molly and Juliet. "You don't think you might be pregnant again, do you?"

"No," she answers quickly, then pauses to think. "Wait, when was my last period?" She pulls her phone out of her pocket. "It was in January."

"Friend, I don't know how to tell you this, but it's March," Madison says with a chuckle.

Tyler nods. "That it is indeed. I guess I better stop and get a test on the way to work. This won't be the first pregnancy test I've taken in the bookstore bathroom."

"You probably got pregnant at the beach when we went. You were high on salty air and seashells and had a quiet moment with your husband for the first weekend in ages," I suggest.

Tyler looks at her phone again. "You're absolutely right. According to the period tracker on my Apple Watch, I was definitely ovulating while we were there. Perfect."

"What's Andrew going to say?" I ask.

"He'll be thrilled, and I will be too. Once I get over the initial shock of it all," she admits. "We wanted to have at least one more. I just thought we'd wait until she was a little older. Out of diapers would have been ideal."

"You hear that, Molly? You have like eight months to get potty trained. We have some work to do," Madison says. "Let's get down to business."

* * *

"I just want to go on the record and say that planning a baby shower after the baby is born is a genius idea," I say to Emilee as she hands me baby Zach.

"Right? No dumb games or guessing the gender. Just baby snuggles in exchange for diapers and wipes," she agrees. "Plus, now I don't have to deal with every person in Fawn Creek randomly showing up at my door wanting to see him at the most inconvenient times."

"Exactly. And if they want to hold your baby, they should at least pay the price of admission with gifts."

"Holy cow," Avery says, wearing a blush-pink maternity dress with a denim jacket. Her own belly makes her look like she could pop any day now. "Emilee, who planned this shower? It's spectacular."

We pause to take in the Sandstone Event Center. In one corner, a blue, white, and green balloon arch frames giant wooden blocks that spell ZACH. Beneath the arch is a white wicker loveseat, just big enough for a guest to sit and hold the baby while Emilee poses next to them for photos.

Every table is topped with a mason jar filled with white roses, eucalyptus, and baby's breath, each tied with a tag holding one of Zach's newborn photos. The gift table is already piled high, and a copy of Where the Wild Things Are waits for guests to sign with sweet messages for Zach.

Emilee smiles shyly. "I did. It's probably silly to plan my own baby shower, but I've been gone so long and don't have a lot of friends in Fawn Creek anymore."

I hold up a hand. "Excuse me. What am I, chopped liver?"

Emilee rolls her eyes. "You're more than my friend. You're my sister. But your life is busy, and I wasn't going to ask you to throw me a party. I mean, you literally just spent last weekend moving Eric and Carson into your house. You don't have time for random party planning."

I frown. "Well, you could have. I'd have done it in a heartbeat. But honestly, I'm glad you didn't because I could never have made something this beautiful. Em, I really think you should open a party-planning business. You'd be incredible."

She frowns. "I don't know. Everyone has Pinterest. They can just as easily look things up and plan it themselves. No one around here is going to pay for something as frivolous as a party planner."

"Who's a party planner?" Tyler asks, joining us.

"Emilee needs to be," Avery says before I can answer. "She planned this, and it's incredible."

"You did all this?" Tyler asks, looking around in disbelief. "With a three-week-old?"

Emilee nods, cheeks pink. "I had a lot of downtime while I was resting after surgery. If it makes you feel any better, I didn't do any heavy lifting."

"Holy hell. Are you for hire? I'd love to have you help me with Avery's shower," Tyler says.

"I don't need a shower," Avery groans. "Isn't it weird to have a shower when you already have a baby? I still have all of Juliet's baby stuff in the attic."

Tyler rolls her eyes. "Yeah, for one baby. You're about to have two. And you're having a boy and a girl. You're going to need boy clothes."

Avery waves her off. "Girl, I am a master shopper. Clothes are not a problem."

"Then let people buy you diapers. We can do a diaper-and-wipe shower," Tyler says, determined. "You can argue all you want, but we're still having one. I've already booked this place for two weeks from now, and I'm hiring Emilee to help me."

"Oh, I... I'm not really qualified..." Emilee starts.

"Not qualified? Look around! You're absolutely qualified." Tyler digs a pen from her purse and scribbles her number on a napkin. "Please help me. I have an eighteen-month-old, a business to run, and a husband who owns one too. I can't plan anything like this. But you can."

"Sounds to me like you birthed a new baby and a new business," I say with a wink.

"Here goes nothing," Emilee replies cautiously.

* * *

"Honey, I'm home!" I call through the house, kicking my shoes off in the entryway and dropping my keys on the table. "Anyone here?"

I pause and wait, but no one answers. Instead, I hear faint chatter coming from the backyard.

I make my way through the house and step onto the back patio to find Eric, Carson, and Piper crouched down in the dirt. They are so busy digging they don't even notice me.

"Hey, what are you guys doing?" I ask.

"Oh no! She's home," Piper groans. "The surprise is ruined."

"Don't look!" Carson shouts, jumping between me and his dad. "We're not ready!"

Quickly, I cover my eyes. "Sorry, I didn't know. Want me to go back inside?"

Eric laughs. "No, you had perfect timing. Come take a look."

I uncover my eyes and carefully make my way across the yard, still barefoot from when I kicked off my shoes. "What are you guys up to?"

"We're making a garden," Carson says proudly.

"We're going to grow strawberries and sunflowers and tomatoes and zucchini!" Piper adds excitedly. "But you aren't allowed to water it because you aren't a farmer like we are."

"Oh. Is that so?" I ask with a chuckle, glancing at Eric.

He stands from his crouched position on the ground. "I hope this is all okay with you. It's such a beautiful day, so the kids and I decided it was the perfect time to get things ready for our summer garden."

I shake my head. "I don't mind at all. I love it, actually. I can't wait to eat fresh veggies all summer, especially knowing I won't be in charge of keeping the plants alive."

Eric wipes his hands on his jeans and leans over to kiss me, careful not to get my dress dirty. "I'll happily take care of the dirty work. You bake the bread and I'll grow the veggies."

"So, Piper, is this why you didn't want to go to the baby shower with me?" I tease.

She shrugs. "No, I didn't know we were gardening until after you left. I just didn't want to go because babies are annoying. They cry too much. And Kate wasn't going to be there anyway."

I shake my head, smiling. "Well, I think you had more fun than you ever would have going with me."

Eric slips an arm around my waist and pulls me close. "We had a great time."

Carson and Piper beam up at us, proud of their garden. I rest my hand on Eric's and whisper, "I love this. All of it."

For a moment, I think back to the conversation I had with Sierra in August, when I confessed that Zach and I had dreamed of having a couple of kids and a house on the edge of town with a garden and chickens. Back then, that dream felt impossible.

But here I am, in that life, with this family, this messy little backyard full of laughter and love.

Chapter 29

"Okay, I think everything is ready to go," Emilee says, pacing as she makes last-minute adjustments to Avery's baby shower.

"Oh my gosh, Emilee! Two peas in a pod? This is the cutest shower theme I've ever seen!" I gush as I step through the door with Piper behind me. I place my gift on the table next to the door and pause in front of a sign that says *Peas, take a picture for the guest book.* I look at Emilee for an explanation.

"Use the Polaroid camera for a selfie, then sign it. I'll stick it in the guest book later," she explains.

"Adorable," I say, pausing for a photo with Piper. I lean down and write a note to Avery on the photo and leave it on the table to develop as Tyler enters with a tray of sugar cookies shaped like pea pods.

"She's a genius isn't she?" Tyler asks me with a wide grin. "I just told her to pick a theme and send me a bill."

"That honestly sounds dreamy," I admit. "Party planning is stressful and, despite my best efforts, it never turns out the way I want it to."

"It was the dreamiest. She didn't charge me nearly enough either, but I'll be fixing that. Every detail of this party is perfect, from the balloon arch with the giant pea pod attached to the hand-painted banner behind it. She has outdone herself,"

Tyler continues.

Avery walks through the door, pausing to take in the décor. "Oh, Emilee, I love it. This is the cutest shower I've ever seen in my life."

"And to think, you didn't even want a shower," Tyler reminds her. "You would have missed out on all this if we had listened to you."

"I know. I'm glad I didn't listen. I love any chance I can get to hang out with you girls. You are truly the best friends I could ask for," Avery says, tearing up just a little. "Sorry, pregnancy hormones."

"Mom, can we have a snack?" Piper asks as she, Kenzi, and Kate make their way over.

"Yes, help yourselves," Emilee says. "There is plenty for everyone."

"Do not make a mess," I warn, plopping into a chair next to Madison. "And don't get too much. Piper, you already ate before coming," I remind her.

"You girls too," Madison warns her children.

"They're fine," Emilee waves us off. "We seriously have plenty."

"You know as well as I do that Piper is a little feral," I joke. "Boundaries are a good thing."

* * *

"Okay, everyone!" Tyler says, standing in front of the balloon arch after the last of the guests trickle in. "I just want to thank you for coming today to celebrate Avery and Derek and their twins, Baby A and Baby B."

"Baby A and Baby B?" An older woman mimics. "Is that what

you're going to name them?" She shakes her head. "You kids these days and your weird names."

Avery's mom, Julie, holds up a hand to stop her. "No, Mildred. That's just what we are calling the babies right now until they decide on names."

Mildred raises a brow, looking even more annoyed. "They haven't named them yet? What are they waiting on?"

"Oh my gosh," Sierra says, leaning into me. "Who is this lady and who invited her?"

I whisper back, "She is a woman that Avery's mom goes to church with. The entire congregation was invited. And Mildred is not one to miss a baby shower."

"She needs to learn to keep some thoughts to herself," Sierra mutters.

"Agreed. But where she lacks in a filter, she makes up for in great gift giving."

"Anyway," Tyler continues, ignoring Mildred and her stink eye, "Avery is not a huge fan of baby shower games, and to be honest, I don't know anyone who is. So instead, we are going to do things a little differently today. Think of this as more of a mingle shower. There are lots of delicious foods to eat, including the charcuterie board over on the west wall." Tyler motions toward the table. "There are also cookies and cupcakes for dessert. We have coffee, tea, water, and lemonade to drink. After you finish eating, head over to the onesie decorating station. We have a vinyl cutting machine if you want us to heat-press a design, or you can do it the old-fashioned way and hand-paint a design. There's also a balloon arch for photos, a selfie guest book, and cards for you to leave your advice for Avery and Derek as they learn to navigate their new life as parents of twins."

"There you go, Mildred. I bet you'll enjoy that," I mutter as Julie shoots me a mom look from across the room. Luckily, Mildred does not hear me.

"So, have fun. Enjoy this incredible party that was planned by our expert party planner, Emilee," Tyler says, gesturing toward her Vanna White style. "Her business is called... what's your business name, Em?"

"Heartland Event Co.," Emilee says shyly to the audience.

"Do you have a Facebook page yet?" a girl from a nearby table asks, as she scrolls through her phone. "I can't find it."

Emilee pauses. "Um... not yet. But I'll get that going right now."

"Perfect," Tyler says, nodding. "We are going to let Emilee go do that. You guys enjoy the party, and thanks again for coming. We will start opening gifts in just a little while."

* * *

"Holy crap," Derek says, making his way into the event space as the last of the guests trickle past him. "Avery... how are we going to fit all of this stuff into our house?" He looks at the pile of gifts Avery unwrapped this afternoon.

"The same way we are going to fit two more humans into our house. With a hope and a prayer," she replies with a nervous laugh.

"Looks like you're going to have to do another add-on," Andrew says. "I know a good contractor."

"Well, you did a good job last time," Avery shrugs. "But I'm not sure if we have room to build anywhere but up at this point."

"We could probably figure something out," Andrew assures her.

"After the babies are here and you are thinking clearly again," Tyler adds with a wink.

Madison shakes her head. "Man, I'm so excited about all these new babies. Avery's will be here soon, and then it'll be Tyler's turn."

"Wait. What?" Avery asks, looking at Tyler. "Are you guys trying again? What did I miss?"

Andrew turns to look at Tyler with a raised brow. "You didn't tell her?"

Tyler lets out a heavy sigh. "No. I haven't told her yet. I wanted today to be all about her," she says, shooting Madison a look.

Madison covers her face. "Oh my gosh, Tyler. I'm so sorry. I didn't mean to tell your secret. I just figured since you two are best friends, she would have been the first to know."

"I hadn't even told you and Ava the results of the test yet," Tyler groans.

"Ava knew before me, too?" Avery's eyes dart around the room.

"Ava and Madison only knew that I was throwing up when we took Molly to the beach," Tyler argues.

"And then we played detective and found that Tyler was ovulating during our group trip. We encouraged her to get a test. But she did not tell us the outcome. Well, she didn't tell me at least," I defend myself, holding up my hands.

"Well, she didn't tell me either," Madison says. "But the whole thing was kinda obvious, so I just assumed it was positive."

"I was hoping by not telling you guys that you would assume

it was negative and I could hold off on telling Avery until after the shower," Tyler confesses. "I still feel bad because my water broke at Juliet's second birthday party and I did not want a second one of Avery's parties about me."

Avery shakes her head and rests her hands on her belly. "Ty, I told you I was so glad your water broke at the birthday party because now Molly and Juliet are birthday twins. And I would have loved to be the first to at least get confirmation about your test. I am your best friend after all." She pauses. "I know my hormones are out of whack these days, but I swear the worst thing that would have happened would have been me crying for joy."

Tyler makes her way over to Avery and bends down to put her arm around her. "Hey, Avery, guess what? I'm having a baby."

"What! That's so exciting! I'm so happy for you," Avery says with a genuine smile.

"I knew you would be."

"I can't wait to add one more baby to this crazy mix," Avery tells her. "And I really mean it."

Chapter 30

"Mom! I can't figure out my dress!" Piper calls down the hall from her room. "I'm stuck!"

"Coming!" I answer, glancing at Eric, who's holding up two different dress shirts, waiting for my decision.

"The green one," I tell him, placing my curling iron on the table and heading to Piper's room.

I find her with her head and one arm crammed through an armhole, and an exasperated look on her face. "Oh, kid, how'd you do that?" I ask, gently lifting the dress back over her head.

Once she's free, I straighten the straps and try again. "Arms up, please."

She obeys, and we get the dress on in one shot. She turns for me to button the back as I smooth out her hair.

"You look so pretty," I tell her, smiling at her reflection in the full-length mirror. "And thank you for wearing this without a fight."

Piper, who usually avoids dresses, beams. "Well, it is really cute. And it's twirly like my dance uniform." She spins in a quick circle to demonstrate.

"You're going to look so cool out on the dance floor."

"Are you going to dance with Eric at the wedding?" Piper asks.

"Well, I sure hope so. He is my date, after all."

"Do you think you and Eric will get married one day?" She sits next to me on the bed, curious.

"Would you like that?" I ask.

She nods. "Yes. I really like Eric, and I think I'd like him to be my dad. And Carson could be my brother. I'm glad they moved in with us. I like having a brother. Maybe I could have a sister one day, too."

I smile warmly and pull Piper into a hug. "We'll see, kiddo. We'll see."

* * *

"Madison and Bryan have prepared their own vows, so they will share them at this time," Pastor Dewitt announces to the wedding guests in the church sanctuary.

"Bryan, go ahead."

Bryan looks over the crowd before clearing his throat. "Madison, from the moment I met you, I knew I had found someone special. Someone strong, beautiful, creative, and just the right amount of chaotic. And I still can't believe I'm lucky enough to spend the rest of my life with you. Today and every day, I promise to love you with everything I have inside me. I promise to love your girls as if they were my own, because as far as I'm concerned, they partially are. I promise to never roll my eyes when you want to paint something pink, even when it's the front door and I know the guys are going to make fun of me for it."

Madison lets out a small giggle that can be heard across the church before Bryan continues.

"I promise to never complain about your ever-growing wardrobe... or the one belonging to your porch goose. I promise to play ball with Kate and let Kenzi paint my nails, and to teach both girls how to drive so you don't have to do it. And more than anything, I promise to keep showing up for you, and for our family. I will choose us and choose you every day for the rest of my life."

Madison quickly wipes a tear from her eye and lets out a nervous laugh. "How am I supposed to beat that?"

"It's not really a competition," Pastor Dewitt tells her.

"Yes it is," Bryan replies with a teasing smile.

Madison takes a deep breath and begins. "Okay, here we go. Bryan, the first time we met, you immediately came to my rescue, literally. One of my girls took a tumble on Main Street in the middle of the tree lighting festival. Before I could even react, you scooped her up and somehow convinced the town pharmacist to unlock the drugstore after hours to get her a bandage. I should have known then that I was in trouble."

She pauses to smile up at him.

"You weren't just Avery's helpful brother. You were steady, kind, and reliable. You're the kind of man who sees what needs to be done and does it instead of waiting for someone else to act. I promise to love you with my whole heart through the chaos, the quiet, and everything in between. I promise not to get too mad when you track grease through the house and dry your stained hands on my decorative towels. I promise not to smother you when you snore loud enough to shake the windows. And I promise to love you even when we're old, even though, let's be honest, you'll get there much sooner than I will."

The entire congregation laughs softly.

Madison continues. "I mean, you rebuilt a Volkswagen for me so I could live out my dreams of driving around town, causing people young and old to punch one another. I love you, Bryan, and I'm so glad you came to my rescue that day, because whether you see it or not, you've been saving me ever since."

* * *

"The wedding was perfect!" I say to Madison as we, along with the rest of the wedding party, gather in front of the church for group photos following the ceremony. "And the vows! I laughed. I cried. Ten out of ten."

"Seriously, it was perfect. You and my brother... you just make so much sense," Avery chimes in, pulling her into a hug.

Madi beams and reaches out to squeeze each of our hands. "Thank you both for being up there with me today. Avery, especially you. I know the last thing you want right now is to stand."

Avery shakes her head. "You're worth every second of my swollen feet. But also, thank you for letting me wear flip-flops. I'm just glad the babies stayed put this long."

"Me too," she agrees. "Let's have Kari finish up the photos with you two so Avery can elevate her feet and Ava, you can get back to Eric."

"Alright, folks, if you're here tonight with someone you love or merely someone you tolerate it's your time to shine and join the bride and groom out on the floor." The DJ's voice crackles smoothly over the sound system.

One by one, couples begin to stand. First, Madison's parents.

236

Then a barefoot Avery and Derek.

"That's you," Piper says, tugging on Eric's shirt sleeve. "You and my mom have to go dance."

"Have to, huh?" I ask.

"Yeah, the guy with the microphone said so," Carson chimes in.

"Well, if the guy with the microphone says so..." Eric holds his hand out to me. "We probably better do this."

I smile softly. "We probably should."

As "I Cross My Heart" by George Strait plays over the speakers, Eric and I join the rest of the couples on the floor. I rest my hands on his shoulders, and he places his own on my hips. For a long moment, we sway back and forth, not speaking, just looking into each other's eyes. I can't fight the goofy grin on my face, and I see him struggling to do the same.

"It's perfect, isn't it?" Eric asks, leaning down and resting his forehead against mine.

"What?"

"You. Me. Us. This. For so long, I thought I was destined to be alone. Supposed to just focus on raising Carson and providing for him. But then I found you, and you gave me hope again."

I stand on tiptoes and lightly kiss Eric's waiting lips. "I love you, and I agree. You are exactly what I've been waiting for all these years. And you were worth the wait."

Chapter 31

"Happy Mother's Day!" Piper and Carson shout as they come barreling into my bedroom, with Eric trailing behind, carrying a bed tray.

I open one eye and press against the bed to sit up. "Good morning," I say groggily. "What's this?"

"We made you breakfast in bed!" Piper announces proudly. "Eric helped a little bit."

"Just a little?" I ask, raising a brow.

"Yep!" Carson replies. "I put butter on your toast and put the strawberries on your plate. And Piper poured the orange juice and got you a fork. Daddy just made your eggs."

"Well," I laugh, "you all did a great job. It looks delicious."

"And we got your presents!" Piper adds, handing me a gift bag.

I peek inside and pull out two homemade cards, as well as a framed picture of the four of us. "Oh, you guys, I love it."

"It's for you to put on the fireplace," Piper explains. "It's our whole family."

"It's perfect," I tell them, placing the frame down and picking up the cards. First, Piper's.

The front reads *Happy Mother's Day*, adorned with a rainbow, flowers, and a giant sun in the corner. Inside, it says: *I love you.*

You're the best mommy ever. Love, Piper.

I pull Piper into a hug. "Thank you! Did you write this all by yourself?"

"Yep!" she says proudly. "I didn't even need help with the spelling."

"That's great! I love it." I set her card beside the frame and pick up Carson's card.

His also reads *Happy Mother's Day* across the front, with a drawing of the four of us holding hands.

"Oh, this is a great drawing," I tell him. "You got my hair just right."

"I worked really hard on it," Carson admits.

"I can tell," I assure him as I open the card to read the inside. *I love you. Will you please be my mommy?*

I read the words aloud, my heart swelling, and turn to him. "Of course I'll be your mommy, Carson. I already feel like I am." I pull him into a tight hug.

Eric clears his throat and slowly lowers to one knee. "Well, I guess the last thing we need to do is make it official." He pulls a ring box from his pajama pants pocket and flips it open.

"Ava, will you please do me the greatest honor of my life and marry me?"

"Please say yes!" Piper begs, folding her hands in prayer alongside Carson, their bottom lips pouted in perfect synchronization.

I laugh through happy tears. "Of course I will. Yes. I'll marry you."

Epilogue

Emilee walks through our backyard with a clipboard in hand, directing her two teenage boy employees where to set up the folding tables and chairs. "Right there. Perfect," she says with a thumbs up. "Now, if you guys can grab the plastic totes out of the trailer and set them on the patio, that'll be great."

"What can I do?" I ask, making my way toward Emilee, nearly dodging the boys as they rush past to fetch decorations.

"You can go sit down and put your feet up. You should be resting. Let me do the work," Emilee says. "You already spent the last month getting settled into your new house. The least you can do is let me take care of your shower."

"Ava's never been one to sit still for long," Madison reminds her. She kisses her one-year-old son, Brycen, on the forehead, then bends to place him in the large outdoor playpen set up for the kids.

"Oh, don't I know it," Emilee says, shaking her head. "You'd think by now she'd know to leave the details up to me. I am, after all, the owner of the number-one party planning business in Southeast Kansas."

"You'd think so, but if she hasn't changed after all these years, she's not going to now," Sierra says as she walks through the gate with Cody beside her. Tyler and Andrew follow close behind.

Tyler is pulling a wagon filled with baby gifts while Molly toddles after them. Andrew has their new baby, Rowen, strapped to his chest in a carrier.

"I can't believe you already have a pen full of chickens, your garden mapped out, and the house unpacked," Sierra continues. "How do you run your business, grow a baby, start a homestead, and still find time to sleep?"

I roll my eyes and grin. "I sleep plenty. Eric just so happens to be a great farmhand. What are you guys doing here so early? Surely you didn't come all this way ahead of the party just to make fun of me for my inability to sit still."

Sierra reaches out to touch my growing belly. "Well, the boys made brisket for the party, so they needed to be here early. We just tagged along. Hope that's okay."

I nod. "Of course."

"I might task you guys with making her sit down and rest while I finish setting up," Emilee says, shaking her head.

"I guess I could go inside and see what Kate, Kenzi, Piper, and Carson are doing," I suggest.

"Minecraft," Avery laughs as she makes her way out the door, followed by Derek. They're each carrying one of their toddlers.

Nora, their daughter, looks more like Avery every day. Her curly hair is tied in pigtails, and she's sporting a hot pink romper. In one hand, she clutches a baby doll she's been dragging everywhere lately.

Henry, their son, has dark hair like Derek and the cutest little fat rolls on his thighs and belly. Derek can't resist dressing that kid in tiny T-shirts and cargo shorts, no matter how much Avery rolls her eyes.

"Juliet's been sucked into the game right along with them,"

Avery adds. "At least the kids will stay occupied for a while."

"What a baby shower," I laugh. "Maybe we should've done a Minecraft theme instead." I glance at my friends. "Thank you all for being here and for putting in all this work. Our baby girl is already so loved. I can't wait to meet her."

"Listen, you had me sold as soon as I heard it was a Baby Q. BBQ and tiny baby shoes? Sign me up," Madison laughs. "I'm just so glad to see you and Eric finally welcoming a new baby of your own."

Eric walks across the yard and pulls me into a hug. "I know it. Our family will finally be complete.

I nod, looking back at our farmhouse, and the yard full of the people we love. "Yep. In just a few weeks, we'll have his, hers, and ours. And I can't wait to raise this kid right here in Fawn Creek, surrounded by the people we love. Forever. Living happily ever after."

About the Author

Michelle Lynn Ross writes heartwarming romantic comedies set in small-town Kansas, where quirky characters, second chances, and unexpected love stories shine. Her work blends humor, and heart. Perfect for readers who believe in happily ever afters and the magic of community.

You can connect with me on:

🌐 https://michellelynnross.com

f https://www.facebook.com/ThatsWhatShellSaid

Also by Michelle Lynn Ross

There's No Place Like Home

Book One of the Fawn Creek Series

When Tyler Burris's long-term relationship falls apart, she's forced to return to her small hometown of Fawn Creek, Kansas. A place she swore she'd never live again. Her plan? Regroup, then get out fast. But between a rogue rooster, nosy neighbors, and a surprisingly charming (and grumpy) next-door neighbor, Tyler might just discover that what she's been searching for has been waiting for her all along.

Small Town Famous

After escaping a toxic relationship, Avery Thompson is focused on rebuilding her life and raising her daughter solo. But when a new side hustle as a content creator brings unexpected attention (and chaos), she starts to find her spark again. Add in a swoony local cop who sees past her scars, and Avery must decide if she's ready to risk her heart... or let fear hold her back.

Single In A Small Town

After a messy divorce, Madison King is determined to start fresh. New hair, new walls, new life. The only rule? Absolutely no more Bryan Thompson. But in Fawn Creek, where dating options are scarce and secrets don't stay hidden, resisting temptation might be the hardest rule she's ever tried to keep.